Other books by Katherine Hetzel

StarMark
Kingstone

Tilda
of
Merjan

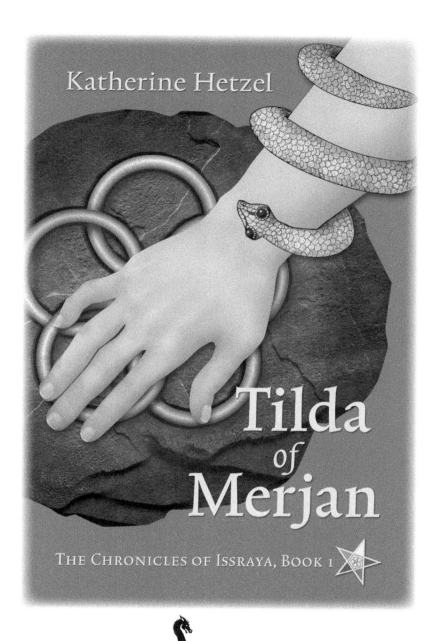

Katherine Hetzel

Tilda
of
Merjan

THE CHRONICLES OF ISSRAYA, BOOK 1

Dragonfeather Books
Bedazzled Ink Publishing Company • Fairfield, California

978-1-945805-99-8 paperback

Cover Design
by

DESIGNS

Dragonfeather Books
a division of
Bedazzled Ink Publishing, LLC
Fairfield, California
http://www.bedazzledink.com

To everyone who stuck with me through the many variations of the story which became—ultimately—Tilda's story. You helped make it what it is.

Acknowledgements

This novel has been a long time in the making, an awful long time. Years, in fact. It was the first story I ever sent off to publishers, and when I look back at the first page now, I cringe at just how bad it was. Understandably, it was rejected.

Over the many years since, I've learnt a lot about how to write stories. This particular story has gone through rewrites too numerous to count, been edited and received feedback from many of my ex-Cloudie and now Denizen friends—among them Debi Alper, Mandy Berriman, Emma Darwin, Jody Klaire, Julie Ironside, Shell Bromley, Gail Jack, Jane Shufflebotham, William Angelo, Matt Willis, and Sophie Jonas-Hill. But there are so many others too; my apologies if I haven't named you all individually. And of course, there's Claudia and Casey at BInk, who have brought that early rubbish story to the end of its journey as *Tilda of Merjan*.

I can't thank all of you enough—Tilda wouldn't be here, as polished as it is, without every single one of you.

I musn't forget the people who've read my earlier novels and asked for more—this time, I promise there will be, because this book is only the start of Tilda's journey. Fingers crossed, there will be four books to follow . . .

And finally, huge thanks to Nick, who lets me get on with my scribbling in the garden room he built 'for writing', and is my better half: 8, 3, 1 x

Chapter 1
Leaving

TILDA STOOD AMID apparent chaos. The prediction of a major storm had forced a great many ships into Merjan City's docks to seek protection; it had also, when it arrived, prevented a lot of others from leaving. But after four days of wind and waves, the clouds had finally cleared, the wind had dropped to a stiff breeze, and now it seemed as though everyone was on the move again.

Including Tilda.

All around her were mountains of crates and boxes and barrels, which the Issrayan cargomen were stacking onto carts ready to take up to the warehouses, or loading onto ships ready for an onward journey. Merjanian merchants bartered as fiercely as any fish-wife for the best deals, shouting up at the merchants from far-off places who stood on the decks of their huge ships. Tilda knew they wouldn't stop shouting until every last grain of rice, roll of cloth, or pottery plate had been bought or sold or had its transport price agreed. Starsmen sat in their designated booths, consulting their charts and tables, preparing to sell personalised starmaps to sailors keen to be certain of their night routes.

A group of weary, sea-stained travellers shuffled slowly past Tilda and she stared at them. Were they fresh off a boat? If so, they must have been at sea during the height of the storm. Thank Power they had not been shipwrecked. It had been bad enough experiencing the storm here, where the two ends of the island curled inwards and Merjan City almost met the Root of Kradlock and protected the city from the worst of the storm's fierceness. Almost, but not quite—the gap between them had still allowed huge waves to come crashing through the Merjan Straits, churning up the normally placid Inner Sea.

Tilda's gaze was drawn away from the travellers towards the fleet of smaller Issrayan Inner Sea boats, tied up for safety during the storm along one entire side of the quay. In a very short while, one of them would take her to Ring Isle. She sighed at the thought of it, and for perhaps the hundredth time, asked the question she already knew the answer to. "Do I really have to go?"

Ma sighed. "Tilda, we've been through this. I can't afford to keep the house, even after selling the business."

All that money, just to pay the Medicians' fees. And it still hadn't been enough. Yes, she knew well enough why she had to go, but as the moment of departure grew ever closer, Tilda racked her brain for something to convince Ma to let her stay. "I don't like leaving you alone."

"I won't be alone. I'll be with Baker Arnal, remember? He's offered me the room above his ovens, and I'll be paid for the bread I make him. I'll soon have enough money to get us back on our feet again. Then you can come home." Ma smiled.

Tilda frowned. She had seen the way the baker had looked at Ma since Pa died, and didn't think it was just Ma's bread making skills he was interested in. "Ma, I really don't want to go."

Ma shook her head. "It's the only way. I'm sorry. I know you're angry and upset, but it's nobody's fault. Not mine, or the Power's, or the mages—"

"Isn't it? They wouldn't use the Power to save Pa."

"We don't know that—"

Tears prickled Tilda's eyes, burning hot, and she feigned a sudden interest in the foreign boats to give herself an excuse to turn her head away from Ma. "A servant told me the mages were too busy trying to help Lord Patricio, and couldn't be disturbed. They told me to go to the Medicians and slammed the door in my face."

"Perhaps they thought the Medicians would be enough."

"Well, they weren't." Tilda's voice wobbled. The hurt and pain of the mages' snub and the loss of Pa formed a tight knot of hot anger in her chest. "They should've used the Power to save Pa, same as they were doing for Patricio. When I get to Ring Isle and see them, I'm going to ask them why—"

"Matilda Benjasson, you will do no such thing!" Ma grabbed Tilda's shoulders and spun her round until they were face-to-face. "You will show the mages respect, like you've been taught, and honour the Power."

Tilda scowled. Why should she? Pa had believed in the Power, honoured it and shown respect for the mages, but it hadn't helped him, had it? Perhaps the Power wasn't the great protector of Issrayans he'd always claimed it to be—just the protector of a chosen few.

Ma was still talking. "Now, your uncle is willing to give you a home and find you work until I'm more settled. Yes, it's on Ring Isle, where Power knows you don't want to be, but that's the way it is and we must accept it." She removed her hands from Tilda's shoulders. "Vanya's coming."

As Tilda watched him weave through the people and possessions piled along the quayside, she supposed she ought to be grateful that Uncle Vanya had arrived in time for the funeral. And that he'd supported Ma so much since. But two days ago, he'd announced that he'd spent too long away from Ring Isle and his work, and it was time to go back. The difference being that this time, he was taking Tilda with him.

She didn't like it, not one little bit, and had resisted for as long as she was able. But the decision had been made, and here she was, waiting to be shipped off to an island in the middle of the Inner Sea. She felt no different to the crates and boxes stacked on the docks; they didn't have a choice in where they went, either.

Vanya reached them too quickly; Tilda would have liked a little longer alone with Ma. She curled her hands into fists and hid them in the folds of her skirt.

"Said your goodbyes?" There could be no doubt that Uncle Vanya and Ma were related; you could see it in the shape of their faces and their colouring. Dark skinned, dark haired, dark eyed. Unlike Tilda,

whose pale skin, coppery curls and green-speckled eyes were more
Pa than Ma.

"Not yet." Ma looked at Tilda. "Are you sure you've got
everything?"

A gust of wind blew several curls across Tilda's face. "Yes."

"Good." Ma reached out her hand as though she would tuck the
hair back behind Tilda's ear.

Tilda jerked her head away and tried not to notice the hurt that
flashed across her mother's face.

Ma let her hand fall to her side. "I'm going to miss you, Tilda.
Write to me, every week. Tell me what's happening, how you're
getting on."

"I won't need to write much. I'll be home soon."

"Hah. Don't get your hopes up," Vanya said.

"What do you—?"

"Don't tell her—"

Vanya held his hand up and spoke loudly to drown out Tilda and
Ma. "Benja left you in a mess, my dear sister, which isn't going to get
sorted any time soon. It's going to take many months, maybe even
a couple of years, until you're able to pay your debts and have Tilda
back in Merjan."

Years?

Tilda gasped. "Ma?"

Ma wouldn't look at her. Tilda stared at her mother in disbelief
and saw for the first time the dark shadows under her eyes, the
strands of silver at her temples which hadn't been there a month
ago. And she understood—properly understood—the situation that
Pa's death had created. Uncle Vanya was telling the truth.

It wouldn't have happened if the mages hadn't refused to use the
Power, a little voice whispered in Tilda's head. It's all their fault.

Anger boiled up, hot and red, inside her, but she forced it down.
All hope of staying in the city evaporated, to be replaced with fierce
determination. She *would* go with Uncle Vanya to Ring Isle. And
when she got there, she *would* find the powermages and ask them for
a damned good reason why they hadn't used the Power to save Pa,

Pa who'd always, *always* believed that the Power was used by them for the good of everyone in Issraya. And if they couldn't explain, well then, she would come home and tell everyone who would listen what frauds the mages were, promising protection and help when they could offer none in reality.

But she wouldn't upset Ma further, couldn't let Uncle Vanya know what she planned to do. They might decide she should stay here after all, and she certainly wouldn't get the answers she wanted in Merjan City. No. She had to be careful about how she did this.

With difficulty, she forced a smile onto her face. "Well, the quicker I get there, the quicker I'll be back. Bye, Ma." She stood on tiptoe to place a swift kiss on Ma's cheek, then walked quickly towards the boats, every muscle straining to keep herself from turning and running back.

"It's the one with the silver fish," Vanya called after her.

She walked past a blue serpent, a green seahorse, a mermaid, and a whale before she spotted the silver fish. She crossed over its gangplank, nodding in reply to the captain's gruff "Mornin.'"

With the deck under her feet, Tilda allowed herself to look for Ma and Uncle Vanya. They were approaching the boat slowly, deep in conversation. It was impossible to hear, but fairly easy to guess, what Ma was saying to Vanya.

"Make sure she eats plenty of vegetables. Don't let her stay up late. Keep her busy so she doesn't miss her father," Tilda muttered under her breath, a fresh stab of grief cutting into her chest at the thought of Pa.

The conversation must be at an end; Vanya hugged Ma, kissed her forehead, then came onto the boat and stood beside Tilda.

"Ready, sir?" the captain called.

"Ready. Ready, Tilda?"

Tilda knew her uncle was waiting for a reply, but she couldn't. There was a lump in her throat that made speaking impossible, and she sought out Ma, the only person who seemed to be standing still among all the busyness of the quay. Focussed on Ma, and on the fact that she was leaving everything she'd known and loved in Merjan

City, Tilda was only vaguely aware of the gangplank being lifted and the ropes being thrown off the moorings. The wind caught the sail and the boat began to slide away from the quay. That's when she started to wave. She waved and waved until she couldn't see Ma anymore and it felt as though her arm would drop off.

"Make yourself comfortable, Tilda. We'll be a few hours on the boat." Uncle Vanya patted her shoulder and walked away, whistling.

Tilda let her arm fall to her side. Standing at the ship's roped edge, she cried then; for Pa, for Ma, for her lost home, and for the uncertain future that waited for her on Ring Isle.

Eventually she scrubbed her cheeks dry and took a deep breath. From this moment on, she had to be strong—especially if she wanted to find out why the mages had refused to use the Power to help Pa.

And if Uncle Vanya mentioned her tears, she'd tell him it was just the wind that had made her eyes water.

Chapter 2
The Silver Fish

THE *SILVER FISH* was typical of an Inner Sea boat. Broad-decked, it had a single mast with a Merjan-blue sail—all that was needed to catch the constantly circling winds—and a raised platform from where the captain would steer. Tilda was used to seeing the little craft scudding over the waves to and from Ring Isle, but she'd never been on one before.

She'd decided not to sit with Uncle Vanya, but to stand instead right at the front of the boat where the deck narrowed and rose towards a high point. On top of the point was the boat's namesake and figurehead; a carved, silver-painted fish. As the little boat cut through the water, the fish was showered in crystal droplets and looked for all the world as though it were real and leaping through the waves.

Tilda's stomach leapt with it. At first, she'd enjoyed the rise and fall of the boat, but after an hour of grey-blue sea, a horizon that moved up and down as well as sideways, and a lump of grey rock that never seemed to get any closer, she was longing for solid ground under her feet again. Her stomach performed a complicated somersault, and she swallowed hard. Was her early breakfast going to make a reappearance? She hoped not. Ma would be so ashamed of her if she set foot on Ring Isle for the first time covered in sick. Perhaps she'd feel better if she stood further back on the deck instead of the very front.

It was strange, to take a step and have the floor drop away from your foot, or have your foot hit the floor earlier than you expected. Unsteady on her feet, Tilda clung to the ropes strung along the side of *Silver Fish* until she was close enough to use the nets thrown over the stack of crates and barrels that, like her, were also heading for Ring Isle.

Uncle Vanya sat, cross-legged, on top of the pile. "Fabulous, isn't it?" he said as Tilda drew level with him. "Makes you feel alive, the sea. Are you enjoying it?"

"Not exactly," she told him through gritted teeth.

Vanya glanced down at her from his high perch. "You do look a bit green around the gills. Just keep taking deep breaths, you'll be right."

Above their heads, the sail snapped taut in an unexpected gust and *Silver Fish* leapt forwards.

Tilda lurched sideways and grabbed hold of a crate of green vegetables. "Oh, Power!" She squeezed her eyes shut and willed her breakfast to stay where it was. If this was sailing, she hoped she didn't have to do too much more of it in the future. How much longer were they going to be on the water?

Vanya laughed. "And this is relatively calm. Imagine what it must be like in a storm. Relax, Tilda. We're in safe hands, aren't we Abram?"

"That we are, sir. Why don't the young lady come on up and steer the Fish for a while? Take her mind off things?"

Tilda opened one eye, swallowed down the bile that had risen in her throat, and looked towards the steering platform.

Abram's smile was a flash of white teeth in his dark beard. "Come on!"

She shook her head. "I don't think so . . . I've never—"

"Sure you can. The wind's steady, 'twas a rogue gust that sent you reeling. It'll be easy now. Just you come on up, nice and slow. In your own time . . ."

What was it in his voice that made Tilda's fingers uncurl and encouraged her to take the first tentative steps towards him? Whatever it was, she found herself climbing the steps onto the platform to stand beside the captain.

Abram nodded his approval. "You get your breath back, lass. Then I'll show you what's what."

As she waited for her heart to stop thumping quite so hard, Tilda tried to guess how old Abram was. Older than Pa, certainly—Pa had never had such deep lines around his eyes, or grey hair. But Pa had also told her once that being out in all weathers aged a man before his time, so perhaps Abram wasn't as old as he seemed. And his age didn't really matter, anyway. What counted was how well he could sail.

Even to an inexperienced sailor like Tilda, it was obvious that Abram was completely at home on the Inner Sea. Was it the way he stood, bandy legs braced wide apart for balance on the gently rolling deck? Perhaps it was his clothes; the breeches tied tight at the knee, the shoes soled in leather and studded with metal for grip on wet wooden decks, or the typical sailor's coat, padded for warmth but sleeveless to allow easier handling of the rudder arm, which he held so easily.

Whatever it was, he made Tilda feel safe. For the first time since setting foot on the boat, she relaxed.

It was as though Abram had been waiting for that exact moment. He smiled and patted the rudder arm. "So, you ready to have a go?"

She took a step closer. "What do I do?"

"Take hold of this first. Can you feel the pull on it?"

She could. The rudder arm—its wood smoothed and darkened with years of use, and warm from Abram's grip—tugged hard in her hands. She nodded and pulled back against the force.

"Not too much . . . that's it. That pull means the wind's filling the sails, and we need to keep 'em full if we want to get to Ring Isle in good time. So you keep it in a position so you feel that tug all the time. All right?"

Nervous at first, but with growing confidence, Tilda watched the sails for any hint of slackness, adjusting the rudder slightly when it did so that the Merjan-blue cloth puffed out full again.

"Now, can you see the large rock to the left of Ring Isle?" As he spoke, Abram took a short pipe and a tobaccy pouch from his pocket.

"Yes."

Abram packed the pipe full and lit it. "You keep looking at that. Keep it in your sights, and we'll be nicely lined up for our landing." He sucked hard to get the tobaccy glowing, and when it was, leaned against the guard rail and looked at her. "So . . . you're Tilda Benjasson, the cobbler's girl? I heard about what happened. A bad thing that, and no mistake. Thoractan ague . . ." He took a deep pull on the pipe and shook his head as he blew out the smoke. "I'm sorry for your loss."

Tilda let his sympathy wash over her and concentrated on the rudder in her hand and the rock in front of her. There was nothing to say, except, "Thank you."

"And now you're leaving your ma behind and heading to Ring Isle."

Tilda managed a nod. She didn't want to have this conversation. Please, Power, let him change the subject.

"Aye, 'tis hard the first time, ain't it? I remember when I left mine for the boats, almos' forty year ago now. I weren't much older than you are now. She's dead now, my ma. Power bless her."

Thank Power, Abram had given her a way to turn the conversation away from herself. Tilda glanced at him, then looked back at her rocky marker. "Do you find it hard to leave your family behind each time you sail?"

Abram snorted. "Me? Family? Nay, no woman'd have me! I'm too in love with my *Silver Fish* and the Inner Sea. I'm not sure I'd want to be tied down. 'Tis a much freer life without wife or children." He shaded his eyes and squinted into the distance. "Less of me, now. We were talking about you, heading off to Ring Isle. A real privilege for you."

"A privilege?" The words came out much sharper than she'd intended. Heat rose in her cheeks.

Abram shot her a look. "You don't think serving the Power is a privilege?"

Tilda searched for the right words. "For some, maybe. I had no choice, not after Pa died. And as the Power didn't save him—" The rest of what she wanted to say was choked off by a sudden surge of anger. She daren't say anything else; it wouldn't be very polite if she did.

"Power don't save everyone. But we all got to honour it if we want what's best for our land." Abram leant over the rail and knocked the remains of his tobaccy into the sea.

"Not me," Tilda whispered. "Not until I find a good reason why the mages wouldn't use it to keep Pa alive."

"Here, let me carry on." Abram slipped his pipe back into his pocket and took the rudder arm from her. "You've done well, we'll make a sailor of you yet."

Yes, she had done alright, hadn't she? Her stomach had settled, and it was good to feel the wind blowing through her hair. Her face, tight from the salt-spray and sun, felt tingly and warm. At ease at last, she sat on the edge of the steering platform, swinging her legs as she watched the waves scud past.

The boat shifted slightly under her.

Vanya yelled and pointed. "We're nearly there. Look!"

Tilda looked. The lump of tall rock she'd set her sights on was fast approaching. Had she really helped to sail them so close to it—and to the rest of Ring Isle? A shiver of excitement ran through her. Oh, how Pa would have loved to see it. He'd told her so much about the place . . .

Tilda jumped down from the platform, and as quickly as she was able to, moved forward to join Uncle Vanya near the silver fish. The boat was close enough now to the island for her to make out the rough surface of rocks and the red eyes of the gannets screaming and wheeling over her head. But that's all there was. Pa had told her about a castle—where was it? Certainly nowhere on these guano-streaked cliffs. Was this stony lump *really* Ring Isle? Or were Uncle Vanya and Captain Abram playing some cruel joke?

Abram must have leaned hard on the rudder arm at that moment, because the boat swung sharply around a ridge of rock jutting out into the sea.

"Welcome to Ring Isle," Vanya said.

Tilda blinked hard. Then her jaw dropped.

There *was* a castle. It looked as though it had grown out of the rocks, it blended so well with the grey cliffs which rose up behind it and swept down on either side too. Hundreds of panes of leaded glass studded the windows set into the walls, dazzling Tilda with reflected light. Under many of the largest windows hung ironwork balconies, looking for all the world like metal bunting strung across the stonework. And high above the vast structure rose six towers, the tallest of them topped with a dome of sparkling crystal.

"Well?" Vanya asked.

Tilda was still drinking in every detail. "It's amazing," she managed to say. "But why is it hidden?"

"It's not, not really. We approach from Merjan City, and the castle's not visible from that direction. It was built on this side of the island to protect it from the strongest of the winter storms. And because we can't land the boats under the cliffs. There's a small natural harbour here."

Oh yes, there, to the right of the castle. She could see it now—a single short quay, jutting out into the water from a tiny shingle beach.

Abram expertly guided *Silver Fish* into the harbour and towards the mooring posts. There were men waiting, half a dozen of them, in a uniform of black tunic and grey leggings. They caught the ropes Abram threw and quickly made the boat secure.

"Welcome back, sir," one of the men called.

"Thank you, Stefan," Vanya shouted over the noise of the gangplank being dragged into place. "Are they back yet?"

"No, sir." Stefan led the other men onto the boat and watched as they began to haul the keepnets from the cargo. "Probably still held up in Merjan after the storm. You've beat them back, but I'm sure they won't mind. Oi, careful with those veg!"

A crate of cabbages teetered for a moment, then crashed to the floor at his feet.

"Who's 'they'?" Tilda asked, ducking when Stefan hefted the fallen cabbage crate onto his shoulder and swung round, narrowly missing her head.

"The powermages, of course," he told her, making for the gangplank at a run.

"They're not here?" Tilda frowned.

Vanya tutted. "Course not. They needed to bury Patricio and select his successor before they returned. Surely you knew that?"

"Yes . . . but . . ." Tilda bit her lip. Of course she'd known. No one in Merjan could have missed the death of their region's powermage. All of the city's blue flags had been at half mast for the last two weeks, and the long funeral procession had been the subject of many a gossiping group. But Pa's death had been closer to home and Tilda had paid that rather more attention.

"The mages actually live away, in their own regions, for much of the year," Vanya continued, "coming back here for the annual Filling Ceremony, or more rarely when Issraya is under threat. See the towers?" He pointed at them. "There are no flags flying at the moment, but as soon as the mages return, they'll be run up. One for each of the regions. Red, green, purple, blue, and yellow. And now the weather's cleared, I bet they won't be far behind us, bringing Patricio's successor for his or her initiation."

Abram had left his steering platform to supervise the unloading. "I always feel better when the flags are flying," he said, glancing up at the towers. "Makes me feel all's right with the Power to see 'em fluttering."

Vanya nodded. "Once they're up this time, they won't be coming down for a while. There's a lot to do after an initiation, so the mages will be staying here for several months. And that means we'll be here that long, too."

Mages . . . Oh, Power. Tilda's stomach gave a lurch that had nothing to do with seasickness. If the mages were going to be around for a few months, she'd have plenty of time to work the best way to approach them and ask her questions.

Uncle Vanya was shaking Abram's hand. "Thank you for getting us here in such good time, Abram."

"My pleasure, sir. Was an honour to have a gentleman of your standing on my little boat."

A gentleman of your standing? What did that mean? Before Tilda could ask, Vanya started across the gangplank. "Come on, Tilda."

She couldn't go without saying goodbye herself. She stuck her hand out. "Thank you, Captain, for getting us here safely. And for letting me sail."

With a laugh, Abram took her hand in his large, rough one, and gave it a gentle squeeze. "You are most welcome, miss." He let go and leaned towards her. "When I get back to the city, would you like me to stop by your Ma's? Tell her you arrived safe?"

"Would you?"

"For sure! And if she scribbles a quick note there and then, why I'll tuck it in my jacket and bring it on my next trip over."

"Oh, that'd be—"

"Tilda!"

Vanya sounded impatient. Tilda glanced over her shoulder; her uncle was waiting at the bottom of a wide flight of steps cut into the rock.

"Coming!" She took a step away from Abram. "Ma'll be at Baker Arnal's. Thank you!" Then she spun round, ran across the gangplank onto the quay, and headed for the steps.

Chapter 3
Aunt Tresa

AS TILDA CLIMBED, she counted.

"Thirteen . . . fourteen . . . fifteen . . ." From various landings on the wide steps, other steps peeled away, each leading to a different entry point of the castle. Why did it need so many? Surely one door would have been enough?

Tilda's pace slowed as her legs protested, but still she was forced to climb. "Seventy-six . . . seventy-seven . . ."

Uncle Vanya was much further up the stairs—had almost reached a large open doorway. By the time Tilda reached the same place, she'd counted one hundred and twenty seven steps and her legs were trembling. Thank Power she didn't have to climb any higher—there were other doors further up than this one.

She took a moment to catch her breath and stared at the huge oak doors—thick as the width of her hand, studded with nails which had turned green from exposure—which stood wide open in front of her. Suddenly, she felt as sick as when she'd stood on the rolling deck of *Silver Fish*. As soon as she passed through these doors, there would be no going back.

"Don't stand there all day," Vanya shouted from somewhere inside.

Quickly, Tilda stepped through the doorway. Inside was a long corridor, decorated in earthy hues of red, brown, and orange. Vanya was already halfway along it, so Tilda set off after him.

To her right were many closed doors in the corridor wall. What lay behind them? To her left, tiled columns framed a series of floor-to-ceiling height windows. The weak winter sun streamed in through them, striping the corridor with light and shade.

Several of these huge windows were open, allowing cold air and the sharp tang of salt to blow along the corridor. What was the view like from up here? Tilda veered towards one of the windows. A peep, that's all she'd need. She stepped onto the balcony outside and—

"Oh, Power!"

The whole world tipped sideways; a wave of dizziness made her stumble. She lunged for the balustrade, steadying herself.

There were holes under her feet! Holes through which she could see rather too much view. Whose idea was it to have a balcony made of swirled metal instead of something totally, utterly, solid?

Between her boots, through the numerous small holes, she could see a toy boat with ants scurrying over its deck.

No, not a toy and not ants; grown men, still unloading *Silver Fish*.

And rocks. Sharp, jagged rocks, which would dash a body to pieces if it fell from this height.

"Not going to fall! Not going to fall!" Tilda's knuckles whitened as she clung even tighter to the balcony, her heart hammering like a sledgehammer against her ribs. Sweat broke out on the back of her neck and trickled down her spine.

She had to get back inside, but she couldn't move.

Using every ounce of willpower, she coaxed the fingers of one hand to let go. She panted, pushing the fear down as she reached behind, feeling for the opening. Where in Power's name was it? The balcony wasn't that big, and she was stretching as far as she could . . .

Her fingertips brushed the edge of the window.

With a gasp, Tilda launched herself backwards towards it. She almost fell into the corridor, and caught hold of the nearest tiled column. She closed her eyes as she hugged it, revelling in its solidity and thankful that she couldn't see that terrible view any longer.

"Seen enough?"

Tilda opened her eyes. Uncle Vanya must have come back for her and seen what she'd done; he was leaning against the wall opposite the open window, one eyebrow raised, arms crossed, waiting.

"Y-yes." Tilda forced herself to let go of the pillar. "Enough to last a lifetime."

"You'll get used to it." Vanya pushed himself away from the wall. "Come on. We're almost home."

Home? No, home was Merjan City. Not here, on Ring Isle.

On legs that felt decidedly wobbly, Tilda followed Uncle Vanya along the corridor until he stopped by one of the doors.

"Up you go," he said, opening it and gesturing her through.

Behind the door was another flight of stairs. Tilda groaned.

"There aren't many this time. Go on, it's worth it."

This time there were only a dozen steps, ending in a small landing and a dark wood door. Should she knock?

Vanya reached past her, turned the handle, and pushed the door open. "Go on in."

Tilda walked into the room on the other side of the door and came to a halt after taking no more than three steps. Had she stepped into a giant kaleidoscope? It looked as though an artist, let loose with a new paintbox, had daubed everything except the white walls with colour. Emerald green couches were piled high with blue-striped cushions. The curtains hanging at the wide window were checked in the brightest of reds, and the floor was covered in scorched orange rugs. There were no clear shades in the wall lanterns. Instead, panes of purple and ruby and golden yellow glass sat between shining brass supports. There was a dresser—painted the palest of blues— on which were displayed a hodge-podge collection of patterned plates and cups, not a single one the same. The tiles on the walls were stained with turquoise and hot pink and lime, and although the stove was black, it was beetle-black-bright. Even the table and chairs, all made from plain, pale wood, had not escaped the eager artist; a pink and red tablecloth covered the table, while the chairs promised a comfortable seat with a selection of plump purple and green cushions.

Vanya squeezed past Tilda, closed the door behind them both, and walked right into the middle of the floor. "Tresa! I'm back!"

A door—one of three in the far wall—crashed open, making Tilda jump. A woman burst out of it and ran straight at Vanya, who caught her up and swung her round.

"Oh, I've missed you," the woman gasped.

"And I you." Vanya planted a kiss on her cheek and set her feet gently back on the floor. "It feels good to be home."

"It feels good to have you back. Here, let me take your coat . . ."

Tilda, still standing near the door, watched in silence. So that must be Aunt Tresa. She barely reached Uncle Vanya's shoulder and was plump and well-rounded, her pale hair braided near each ear and pulled up and over the top of her head like a crown.

Tresa was smiling at Uncle Vanya—it put dimples in her rosy cheeks. "It's been so long. I take it everything went well in Ambak?"

"It did." Vanya threw himself onto a couch. "Until I received a message from Eva."

"Oh? Bad news?"

"Benja died."

Tilda gasped at the bluntness of his words.

Tresa heard. She spun round quickly and stared, open-mouthed, at the girl standing by her front door.

"Um . . . hello," Tilda managed.

Tresa's mouth closed with an audible snap. She crossed her arms over her chest and glared so fiercely, Tilda backed away until the door pressed into her spine and she could retreat no further. Eventually, after several long, uncomfortable moments, Tresa spoke, every word clipped short. "Who is this? Explain, please, Vanya."

Vanya jumped up. He took Tresa's elbow, and steered her into a corner. He kept his voice low and spoke close to Tresa's ear, but Tilda still caught a few of the whispered words.

"Tilda . . . Benja dead . . . debts . . . too much to cope with . . . family . . . needs support . . . not for long . . . look after her."

Tresa cast a frown over her shoulder, in Tilda's direction. "But—"

Uncle Vanya straightened up. "No buts, Tresa." He wasn't whispering any more. "This will be Tilda's home for the foreseeable future, longer if I can secure her a job here too. Please, help her to feel welcome." He left Tresa and walked over to Tilda. "Come." He took her arm and gently drew her into the room until she stood only an arm's length away from her obviously unhappy aunt.

Before anyone could say anything, there was a knock at the door.

"Brought the young lady's trunk up, sir," someone called.

Tresa stepped right around Tilda and hurried over to the door. "Bring it in. Just leave it there," she added, pointing to the floor when one of the grey-uniformed men entered, carrying Tilda's box on his shoulder. When the door closed behind him and there were only the three of them again, Tresa shoved her hands deep into her skirt pockets. "Well. What do we do now?"

"I suggest that Tilda has something to eat and unpacks, while I check on how things have been in my absence," Vanya said.

"Do you have to go straightaway?" Tresa actually pouted. "You've only just got home."

"You know how it is, Tresa." Vanya chucked her under the chin. "I'll be back in a couple of hours, that's all."

He left, leaving Tilda and Tresa staring at each other over the dumped trunk.

Tresa spoke first. "Are you hungry?"

Was she? Tilda's stomach had tied itself into knots when she'd seen Tresa's reaction. She didn't think she could eat a thing because of it. But her stomach obviously had other ideas; it gave a loud rumble at the prospect of food.

"A little," she admitted.

"Well, best get some fritters fried up then."

Half an hour later, after a generous helping of bacon and onion potato cakes eaten under the watchful eye of Tresa, Tilda pushed her empty plate away. She'd been hungrier than she thought.

"They were good," she said. "Thank you."

"You're welcome." Tresa wiped the frying pan clean and set it on the pan rack with a bang.

Tilda toyed with the tassels hanging around the edge of the tablecloth. Was Tresa angry because Vanya had brought her here without any warning? If so, she ought to try to clear the air between them. "I'm sorry you didn't know. About Pa. Or about me coming here."

Tresa turned and looked at Tilda. Then she gave a sigh and sank into the chair opposite. "No, I'm sorry, Tilda. You've been through a hard time already, you don't need me to make it harder. Your uncle's a good man, but impulsive. I find it hard at first when he thrusts a problem upon me."

So now she was a problem? Tilda dropped her chin to her chest to hide the flush of shame she knew was creeping over her cheeks. She should've stayed with Ma, not come here if she was going to be in the way.

A warm hand covered hers where it lay on the table, and she looked up.

"Shall we start again, eh?" Tresa smiled, patted Tilda's hand and then whipped the dirty plate away to the sink. "I really should think more, before I open my mouth. Forgive me?"

If Aunt Tresa could apologize, Tilda could forgive. She nodded and leant on the table as she looked around the room again. "This is where you and Uncle Vanya live, then?"

"Aye, our personal quarters." Tresa dunked the plate in a bowl of water and gave it a scrub.

"It's very . . . colourful."

Tresa started to wipe the dripping plate dry. "It is, isn't it? I like colour. Lots and lots of colour." She put the dried plate back on the dresser and flung the drying cloth over a shoulder. "How about I show you the rest of our home?"

"Yes, please." Tilda pushed her chair away from the table and joined Tresa by one of the three doors in the wall.

"This is mine and your uncle's bedroom." Tresa allowed Tilda a brief glimpse inside. Decorated in blues and greens, with only the narrowest of windows, it was like looking into a watery cave. Tresa pulled the door shut and moved on to the next, the one she'd burst out of when Tilda had arrived. "This is my workroom."

A smaller room, this time. Painted white, with a wide window to catch the sun. Beneath the window was a table, covered in lengths of plain fabric and a mountain of coloured threads.

"I'm a member of the Academy of Needles," Tresa explained. "My job here is to decorate furnishings and make repairs when the damp sea air rots the fabrics. I'm working on some cushion covers at the moment, for the new Merjanian mage's rooms." She held up a square of blue with the beginnings of a design worked into it.

Tilda shivered, recognising the half-stitched crossed wands and snake. She'd seen more of that one than she'd wanted to in recent weeks.

Tresa laid the work down and ushered Tilda out. "I'm stitching the insignias of the different academies. I only have the Medicians and I think that's all of them done. Oh, no, there are the Historykeepers too, but that one won't take long." She paused in front of the third door. "This one, well . . . I suppose this had better be yours. It's not very grand, but I think you'll be comfy enough." She opened the door of Tilda's new bedroom.

A deep-piled rug, the colour of ripe peaches, covered most of the floor. Against one wall was a raised brick sleeping platform, topped with a thick mattress. Folded neatly at one end of the bed was an orange and red striped coverlet, and beside it, a pile of orange pillows. A dumpy candle sat in a mirror-tiled alcove above the bed, and next to that hung a painting.

"That's my home!" Tilda crossed the room in an instant and stared at the house in which she'd grown up; the steeply sloping roof with the attic window tucked into its eaves, the diamond patterns of blue and red bricks on the upper floors, and the blue shop door with the oversized brown boot hanging over it.

"I'd forgotten that was in here." Tresa squinted at the painting. "Your mother painted it herself, years ago, when she first got married. Wanted to show her big brother how well she was doing."

Tilda didn't know whether to laugh or cry. Finding the old house here—her home, up until this morning—in the place that she was supposed to call home now . . . Was it good or bad to be reminded of it? A bit of both, she decided. It would remind her of family times, all together, which she knew would be painful—at least for a while. But it would also remind her of how much had been lost, and why she was determined to find out about the mages and how they used the Power.

"Is it alright to leave it here? Or would you prefer me to move it?" Tresa reached for the frame to lift it down.

Tilda caught her arm and stopped her. "No! It's fine, honest. I'm glad it's going to be in my room. Thank you."

Tresa's cheeks flushed pink. "Well, that's all right then. Now, let's drag your trunk in, and you can get yourself unpacked."

Chapter 4

A Second Boat

IT DIDN'T TAKE long to unpack. Tilda closed the lid on her empty trunk and sat on the bed, satisfied with a job well done.

Her coat now hung on a peg beside the door, her boots and best shoes—the last pair Pa had ever made—lined up underneath it. Her clothes were packed into the carved wooden chest at the end of the sleeping platform, along with a few sprigs of sea lavender she'd found in there. Her books were stacked on a shelf near the window, a portrait of Ma and Pa standing next to them. The portrait used to stand on the mantelpiece over the kitchen fire in her old home, but Ma had insisted Tilda take it with her.

At the thought of Ma, Tilda glanced up at the painting. A new family would be moving into that house soon, erasing all traces of the Benjassons' previous life there. Strangers would eat *their* meals in the cosy kitchen. *They* would feed the pigeons which strutted along the roof outside what had been Tilda's attic bedroom window. And perhaps another cobbler would sit at Pa's workbench, making shoes, just like he used to. Tilda's heart twisted and a wave of homesickness brought tears to her eyes. Would there be another little girl, too, who sat beside *her* pa and listened to his stories about Issraya and its Power? How it hurt, to think of that . . .

Tilda closed her eyes, and thought back to what it had been like.

"In a sea full of islands, there's one shaped like a tooth: our very own Issraya." Pa always started his stories that way, threading his needle at the same time. "Now, if the island is a tooth, its crown is Ambak, where there's snow on the mountains year-round and lions, bears, and eagles live alongside the berry farmers. Beneath those mountains are the forests of Pergatt, where it's difficult to know what's treasured more. Their fine timber, or the earth so full of jewels 'tis said you can simply scratch the surface and find yourself a diamant or emeralt. And beneath the forests are the Nargan plains, where farmers grow fat on their harvests and a dragon crawls across the land."

He'd pause then, line up the pieces of leather which would, in his skilled hands, soon turn into a shoe. With the first stitch secured, he'd continue.

"A tooth has roots, don't it? Well, one root of Issraya's tooth curves in from the left, all steep cliffs and hard rock. That's Kradlock. The people there are as hard as the stone from which they build their houses, and they store the bones of their ancestors in the old mines." The thought of those bones had always made Tilda shiver, and she shivered again now, as she remembered. "The other root, Merjan, where we live"—he'd always tweak her nose at that point—"curves in from the right 'til it almost touches Kradlock. But not quite. There's a gap, just big enough to let the boats sail into the Inner Sea or leave to travel across the Outer Sea."

"What's in the middle of the Inner Sea, Pa?" she'd always ask, knowing full well, but wanting to hear him say it anyway.

"Why, another island, slap bang in the middle of The Inner Sea. And that, Tilda, my child, that is where Issraya's Power rises up from the ground, channelled through five silviron rings which the mages, Power bless them, take into themselves to use on behalf of us ordinary folk and—"

A gentle knock on the bedroom door cut Tilda's memories short. She opened her eyes and swiped a hand across her cheeks. No point in crying. It wouldn't change anything. Not now.

Tresa poked her head into the room. "Almost done?"

"Done." Tilda hopped off the bed. "What shall I do now?"

A bell rang, far in the distance.

"Another already," Tresa said.

"Another what?"

"Boat. They'll come thick and fast now the storm's passed, I suppose. The bell's rung from the lookout post, to give folk enough time to meet the boat when it docks. Tis interesting to see them arrive, though." Tresa cocked her head. "Tell you what, why don't you come and have a look from my workroom window while I get a bit more stitching done?"

Tilda bit her lip. "Aren't we really high up? I didn't like it when I looked before, from one of the balconies."

Tresa flapped a hand at her. "Those balconies! Enough to scare the pants off anyone. I don't like them either, and I've got a good head for heights. It's the holes between your feet, isn't it? You'll be fine if you're inside." She put an arm round Tilda's shoulders and steered her into the workroom next door. "Now, I'll finish this off"—Tresa picked up the Medicians' cushion cover and sat at the table—"while you have a look and tell me what you see."

Did she dare? She didn't want to feel that awful dizziness again. But there's solid ground under your feet this time, Tilda reasoned with herself. It'd be no different to looking out of the attic window at ho . . . back in Merjan City, but higher, that's all. And how many times had she leaned out of *that* window, to see the boats coming in through the Merjan Straits?

Tilda took a breath, opened the window, and leaned out. Far below, another of the Inner Sea boats was turning into the harbour. There must be something different about this one though; it had created quite a stir in the harbour, judging by the number of uniformed servants running towards it.

"There are people on the boat," Tilda told Tresa. "And some cargo." She watched the boat moor up and counted the passengers as they disembarked. "There are . . . eight . . . no, nine. Nine passengers, all coming up the steps now." She watched for a moment or two, then frowned. "They're all taking different staircases." She turned back into the room. "Why don't they all come up the same way?"

"Depends where they need to get to in the castle, that's all," Tresa said, head bent over her stitching.

"Oh." Tilda leaned out of the window again. To her disappointment, the passengers had all moved out of sight. There was only the boat and the cargomen to see now. For some reason, the boat caught her attention and held it. There was something . . . extra on it.

"This boat's flying a flag," she realised aloud. "A black flag with grey circles. It looks like—"

"What? Oh, Power preserve us!" Tresa jumped to her feet, threw the cushion cover down, and dashed out of the room.

"What is it? What's wrong?" Tilda hurried after her aunt, but Tresa had ducked into her bedroom and before she could follow, footsteps pounded up the stairs.

The main door crashed open, and Vanya burst through it, panting. "They're back! Where's my coat?"

"I've got it, I've got it. No need to shout." Tresa appeared from the bedroom, carrying a red coat.

"I wasn't ready," Vanya muttered as she helped him into it. "I should have been—"

"It would have been worse if you'd not been here at all, but he'd have understood, I'm sure, given the circumstances." Tresa smoothed the fabric and stood back, inspecting Vanya. "Just thank the Power you're here now."

Tilda stared at her uncle. The knee-length red coat he'd put on had a design embroidered on the left chest: five grey rings, interlocked in a circle. The same symbol which had been on the flag on the newly arrived boat. With a jolt, she realised what it meant. How could she have not recognised it? She pointed at it with a shaking finger. "But that's . . . Why have you . . . ? Uncle Vanya, you've got—"

Tresa interrupted her. "Are you going to take Tilda with you now or will you wait?"

A giant hand squeezed Tilda's stomach when they both turned their heads and studied her. What in Power was going on? Who would Uncle Vanya be taking her to see? And why did his coat have—

"I don't know. He'll have a lot to think about," Vanya muttered. He rubbed his chin thoughtfully. "He might not welcome the distraction."

Tresa nodded. "But you know how he likes to know everything that's going on. He won't thank you for springing Tilda on him at an inconvenient time. Is it better to get it over with?"

Vanya appeared to come to a decision. "Smarten yourself, Tilda, quickly. And be on your best behaviour. Or else."

Tilda smoothed out the creases in her travel-crumpled skirt and straightened her shirt collar, wondering who this mysterious person could be. It sounded like she was going to find out soon . . . whether she liked it or not.

"You'll do," Tresa said, after a quick inspection. "Now, go with your uncle. Speak only when spoken to, don't stare, and—"

Vanya was already at the door. "Enough, Tresa. We must go. I would not keep him waiting after I've been away from him for so long. Hurry, Tilda."

"Go!" Tresa shooed Tilda out of the apartment.

She took the stairs two at a time in an attempt to catch up with Vanya and called out to him. "Who, though? Who are we going to see?"

"Lord Silviu," Vanya tossed over his shoulder.

"What?" Tilda gasped and almost fell down the rest of the stairs. Lord Silviu? But he was . . . "Powermage of Ambak," she whispered. Why were they going to see him?

"Come *on*, Tilda." Vanya was already in the corridor.

She caught him up, forced into almost running to keep pace with his long strides. "Uncle Vanya, I don't understand. Why are we going to see Lord Silviu?"

"Because I'm his steward."

"His—" Tilda pulled up short. "But . . . but you're just a servant. Cleaning rooms, fetching and carrying . . ."

Vanya took several more strides before he realised Tilda wasn't by his side. With a sigh, he stopped, too. "There's still a fair bit of that goes on, even as a steward. But my primary role is to support the powermage I serve."

Tilda shook her head, not quite believing what she was hearing. If he was a steward to a powermage, well, that explained the rings on his coat, but it had to be one of Issraya's best kept secrets, because Ma had never, ever—

She frowned. "Does Ma know?"

"Of course."

"Then why didn't she tell me?"

A muscle twitched in Vanya's jaw. "Better not to advertise the fact, I've found, because when people find out I'm a steward, they tend to start asking to meet the mages. And in light of your current feelings towards both the Power and the mages, I thought it best to keep you ignorant of the fact."

How could they have kept this from her? Her first day on Ring Isle and she was going to meet a powermage? It meant that she could start asking about Pa straightaway, find some answers... No, actually, she couldn't. If she tried, she'd likely find herself back on the next boat and heading home in disgrace. The best way would be to watch and listen and find out as much as she could about the mages and their use of the Power without alerting anyone's suspicions. Including Uncle Vanya's.

"I miss Pa," she said. "I was angry with them, but I'm trying not to be. Pa was very sick."

Vanya grunted and indicated they should walk on. "Well, try and keep that anger hidden. Show Lord Silviu respect like you've been taught, and perhaps all will be well."

They continued in silence along twisting, turning corridors tiled or carpeted or painted in shades of mainly red. It felt to Tilda as though she was walking inside a giant vein. In fact, apart from Vanya's apartment, everywhere she'd been so far was very red . . . And red was Ambak's colour.

Why hadn't she made the connection before, when she first set foot inside the castle? Did it matter that she was Merjanian, not

Ambakian? She'd better ask her uncle. "You're Ambakian, aren't you?"

Vanya glanced down at her. "Me and your Ma, yes."

"So do you have to be Ambakian to be Lord Silviu's steward?"

"No. The mages choose someone they can trust and work with from anywhere in Issraya. But your Ma and I grew up with Silviu, were the best of friends, and when he was chosen to be the mage of Ambak, he asked me to be his steward. That's all."

"So it doesn't matter that I'm Merjanian?"

"No."

That was a relief. But another worry began to niggle at Tilda. It was one thing to lie to Uncle Vanya, convince *him* that she wasn't angry any more, but could she do the same to a mage? A mage . . . she was going to meet a real, live powermage! She flushed hot and then went cold. Would Silviu use the Power to tell him what she was really thinking and feeling? Her heart thumped hard in her chest.

"What am I going to do?" she whispered.

Chapter 5
Silviu

"RIGHT, HERE WE are." Vanya halted in front of a surprisingly plain door.

Tilda had expected to see ornate carving, or gold or silver painting on the door to a powermage's rooms. Not a simple silver-grey circle, painted on a deep red square.

"Now remember, don't speak unless you're spoken to, but if he does talk to you, you address him as My lord or Lord Silviu. Got it?"

"Got it."

Vanya rapped smartly on the door.

A deep voice called from the other side. "Enter."

Vanya opened the door and gestured Tilda through; she stepped inside.

A black and white striped tiger lay on the floor, snarling at her.

Tilda gasped and jumped back, crashing into Vanya.

"It's only a rug!" he hissed, catching hold of her arm and giving her a shake.

A what? Tilda looked again. Oh. Yes. A rug. She could see that now. Just an empty skin, but with painted glass eyes that were far too realistic for her liking. It must have been a magnificent creature when it was alive. She followed Vanya further into the room, tiptoeing around the unfortunate tiger.

"You'd better get used to it. There's more." Vanya jerked his head upwards. "Silviu is a keen hunter."

Tilda managed to swallow the yelp that rose to her lips when she looked up. Staring down at her from the walls were rows of mounted animal heads; giant cats, tusked boar, deer with and without antlers—even a black bear. And there were others she did not recognise. A lot of their mouths showed some very sharp teeth. She shuddered and dropped her gaze. Looking around the rest of the room was a lot less scary.

The red theme in the decoration continued here, too, most notably in a couple of well-padded and vividly coloured scarlet couches which had been placed close to a large, empty fireplace. One of the couches had a large pile of grey fur laid upon it. Near the single wide window was a desk, its top covered in red leather, the desk chair upholstered to match.

The pile of grey fur suddenly launched itself at Vanya.

Tilda opened her mouth to scream—a bear was attacking her uncle, had grabbed him in its arms.

Vanya thumped it on its back, and grinned when it released him. "Silviu!"

"Vanya," the bear replied.

The scream died in Tilda's throat. Bears couldn't talk. She looked again, and her legs turned to jelly with relief. Thank Power, it wasn't a bear after all. Only a man, wearing a heavy winter coat.

This was Silviu? Granted, he was tall, with hair and beard almost the same colour as his coat, brilliant blue eyes, and skin weathered dark like Abram's, but he didn't look anywhere near as important or extraordinary as Tilda had expected him to.

"I'm glad you're back." Silviu smiled, deepening the creases at the corner of his eyes. "Especially after you had to leave so suddenly." He glanced at Tilda over Vanya's shoulder. "Who's this?"

The strangest sensation came over Tilda when he looked at her. Warmth stole up from her toes and climbed her body until she felt sure her cheeks must be glowing because of it. She was completely enveloped—but in what?

Vanya pulled her forward, his hand heavy on her shoulder. "My niece, Tilda."

Tilda lowered her eyes and dropped a clumsy curtsey. She looked up, and a shiver ran down her spine; Silviu had stopped smiling.

"Your niece?"

Vanya's hand tightened on Tilda's shoulder. "Matilda Benjasson. You remember the message I received when we were in Ambak? From my sister, Eva?"

"Ahh, yes." Silviu nodded slightly. "Her husband . . . Benja, wasn't it? He was ill. Thoractan Ague."

Tilda couldn't help feeling surprised; Silviu seemed to know an awful lot about her Pa, considering she'd been told the mages were too busy to help him.

"Yes. He died. Eva was left in financial difficulties as a result, so I have offered to look after Tilda until Eva is more . . . solvent."

He had made it sound so simple. He'd completely forgotten to say anything about the mage's refusal to come to Pa's aid as a reason for Ma being in the mess she was in.

Tilda clamped her mouth shut, literally biting back the words she wished she could have said, until she tasted iron. Her stomach fluttered.

Silviu was staring at her, frowning slightly. Could he tell what she was thinking? She hoped not. She made a conscious effort to relax her jaw.

"My own daughter without a mother, and another's daughter without a father. The Power did not help in either case."

Had she heard that right? Silviu's voice had been soft, but Tilda was sure he'd said—

At least he wasn't staring at her now, but looking over her head.

"Is Tresa happy with this arrangement, Vanya?"

"She is now."

Silviu nodded. "Very well. Let Tilda stay with you. I take it you will try to find her some way of being useful to Ring Isle?"

"Yes." Vanya gave Tilda's shoulder one last squeeze and let his hand fall.

Silviu nodded again. Then he looked back at Tilda and she jumped. "I think we can do better than that in the short term. Here's your first job, Tilda."

"My first job?"

Vanya poked her in the back.

"My Lord," she added.

"Help me out of this coat, because I'm roasting in it!"

She obliged, staggering under the weight of the fur as Vanya directed her into a bed chamber to the left of the room with the hunting trophies.

If the corridors on the way here had felt like veins, then this room felt like a heart. Tilda gazed round with wide eyes at the huge wood-framed bed—covered in a patch-worked quilt made of fabrics in every shade of red from deepest ruby to bright scarlet—and at the walls, tiled in crimson and gold up to the windowsills. Curtains decorated with red dots and green leaves framed a single large window; to one side of it was a seat hewn from the trunk of a giant tree and a bookshelf made from unvarnished redwood. On the other side of it was a small, practical desk—empty of papers—and an ordinary chair whose seat was covered in blood-coloured velvet.

"Put the coat in there." Vanya nodded towards a redwood wardrobe standing in a corner. "And be careful. That's best oxala fur. Silviu hunted and killed the animal it's made from."

Tilda's feet sank into thick wine-coloured rugs as she crossed the room and did as she was told.

"Hmm." Vanya frowned. "Can't unpack. Trunks haven't made it up here yet. Not sure what else I can do in the meantime. For now, we're done in here."

Back in the other room, Silviu was standing by the window, looking out to sea. Tilda blinked. What was that faint red haze, hanging in the air around him? But then Silviu moved, and the haze disappeared. Tilda blinked again. Had she imagined it? Or was it a trick of the light, some reflection of all the redness in the bedroom?

Silviu threw himself down onto one of the couches with a sigh and stretched out.

Vanya leaned against the mantelpiece opposite. "How did Neesha take it when you were recalled?"

The two men seemed to have forgotten about Tilda. Uncertain as to whether she should remind them of her presence, she stayed by the bedroom door and listened.

Silviu shook his head and rubbed his chin. "I think it's safe to say that my daughter was not at all happy. You know she hoped to have me home until the spring, have us go up to the farm together. Indeed, I'd hoped for that myself, but . . . It's getting harder to leave her behind. Power only knows what she'll get up to this time."

"Abchar won't let her do anything too dangerous, my friend."

"I suppose not." Silviu sat up suddenly. "Do you know he took her hunting last summer? Wanted an oxala coat of her own, he told me. She's a child, for Power's sake!"

So the daughter liked hunting as much as the father, did she? Tilda felt sorry for the wild animals of Ambak.

"I musn't dwell on what's happening back at home, though." Silviu swung his legs over the edge of the couch and stood up. "Things are about to get rather busy."

"The new powermage," Tilda whispered. Vanya must've heard; he shot her a look, and she remembered she musn't speak unless she was spoken to. No one had told her she couldn't listen though . . .

"Who?" Vanya asked Silviu.

"Yaduvir."

"Ah." Vanya's eyebrows shot up into his fringe.

"I know." Silviu ran a hand through his hair. "We thought the same when I received the list of candidates. But I had furthest to travel after receiving the summons to attend Patricio, so Yaduvir had managed to charm the others into supporting him even before I even arrived in Merjan City."

Interesting. It sounded as though Silviu didn't like the new mage. Why?

Vanya laughed. "Of course he hadn't charmed them. It's the Power in each of the initiated mages that ultimately decides, as you are well aware. Think back to your own selection, and what happened with Luisa. Did she succeed, even with all her charms?"

Silviu grunted.

"You just need time to get used to the idea of someone different, after so long serving alongside Patricio."

"Perhaps. I must trust that the Power knows best." Silviu shrugged. "And assuming it does, then tonight is Yaduvir's welcome."

Vanya crossed his arms. "Your trunks had better arrive soon then, otherwise you'll be going in what you've got on."

"Or my oxala coat." Silviu laughed. "Look, why don't you take Tilda back to your rooms? I have some reading to do, and I bet the trunks'll be here by the time you get back."

"You're sure? You don't need me for anything else?"

"Perfectly sure." Silviu smiled at Tilda.

She couldn't help noticing that his eyes didn't crinkle this time— only his mouth moved.

"No doubt I will see you again, Tilda Benjasson."

She nodded. Oh, he would. She'd make sure of it.

Chapter 6
An Extra Pair of Hands

TILDA'S HEAD BUZZED with everything she'd heard as Uncle Vanya walked her back to his rooms. Mentally, she checked off what she'd learnt; that Silviu had a daughter called Neesha, and they both liked hunting. That the Power had apparently helped to choose Yaduvir, a man that neither Silviu or Vanya seemed to think very highly of. And tonight, Yaduvir was going to be welcomed.

Or maybe not, if Silviu didn't like him. It was strange to think that the mages didn't necessarily like each other—especially when they must have to work closely together to decide how to use the Power in Issraya.

Tilda bit her lip. Maybe they didn't always agree. Could that be why they hadn't used the Power to save Pa? She was still trying to puzzle that one out when Vanya dropped her off.

"I'm going straight back," he told Tresa. "Welcome is tonight, so I might be late home."

Tresa looked up from the pan she'd been stirring on the stove and pointed a dripping spoon at him. "You're going nowhere until you've eaten. Sit down."

"Tresa, I can't. I have to—"

"You have to eat, and it's almost ready." She glared at Vanya; he held her stare for a moment, then sighed and sat down at the table. Tresa turned back to the pan and started stirring again.

Tilda sniffed. "It smells good. What is it?"

"Soup." Tresa lifted the spoon again and slurped a pale liquid from it. "Perfect." She took the pan off the stove and transferred its contents to a bright yellow and purple-spotted dish. "Will you set the table, Tilda?"

With the table set, everyone took their places and Tresa ladled out the creamy fish soup. Then she cut thick slices from a squat loaf of brown bread.

Tilda reached for a slice.

"Ah-ah-aaahh." Tresa shook her head. "First, we give thanks. Power of Nargan, feed us. Power of Ambak, water us. Power of Pergatt, enrich us. Power of Merjan, educate us. Power of Kradlock, keep us. Thanks be to the Power for this food. Now, you can eat."

Tilda tucked in. It really was good.

Vanya broke off chunks of bread and dropped them into his soup. "Well, if I'm going to stop long enough to eat, Tresa, you might as well tell me what's been going on here while I've been away."

In between mouthfuls, she told him, but Tilda stopped listening after a while. There were too many names, too much information to digest. And none of it was about the mages or the Power—it was all just day-to-day details of castle life. Then she heard her own name in the conversation.

"Huh?" She looked up.

" . . . start asking soon," Vanya was saying, "about where she might be best put to work. Silviu's happy for her to be here, so that's half the battle."

"You could ask today." Tresa wiped the last of her soup up with a crust.

"I've got more important things to think about today, like the welcome."

Tresa chewed for a moment, swallowed, and leaned back in her chair. "There might not be a welcome."

Tilda stared at her aunt, a spoonful of soup suspended in mid-air over her bowl. Could Silviu really stop it from happening if he didn't like Yaduvir?

"What are you talking about," Vanya snapped. "Of course there will."

"Well, there's been a bout of nasty fever here, while you've been away. There are many who have taken to their beds, 'specially from the kitchen. An extra pair of hands might be well used down there tonight."

In the kitchen? Tilda's appetite disappeared and she lowered her spoon back into the bowl. She knew that Uncle Vanya had intended to find her a job here, but did she really have to start working straight away? And how would she find out anything more about the mages and the Power if all she was doing was baking bread or peeling vegetables or—

"Do you really think they'd take her on?" Vanya slurped his soup loudly.

"Vanya! Manners."

Aunt Tresa sounded cross, but Tilda caught her trying not to smile; she couldn't help grinning herself.

Uncle Vanya dipped his spoon into his bowl, pursed his lips and, with exaggerated care, sucked the soup from the spoon without making a sound. "There."

All three of them burst out laughing.

Tresa swatted him playfully. "Oh, you! I'm serious though, Vanya. Surely there's no harm in trying the kitchen for Tilda?"

"No, suppose not." Vanya nodded slowly. "Tilda, help your aunt to clear up, then we'll take a wander down. They might not need you, but if they do, well . . . Got to be better than sitting doing nothing on your first evening on Ring Isle, hasn't it?"

Tilda sighed. She wouldn't have minded doing nothing. It had been a long day. But it seemed, like in so much that had happened recently, she didn't have much of a choice.

"Yes, Uncle Vanya," she murmured.

The kitchen certainly looked like it needed help when Tilda followed Uncle Vanya into its steamy chaos.

"There's enough of us to manage the cooking, but I could still use you," the plump cook panted as she whipped up a load of egg whites in a bowl. "You can hold a tray, can't you? Without spilling it?" Before Tilda could reply, the cook bellowed, "Harfra, don't put those berries in yet! They need to be stoned first. Stefan! Where are you?"

"Sounds like you're going to be busy. I'll leave you to it," Vanya said, glancing up at the huge clock on the wall. "I must get back to Silviu. I'll see you later. Good luck." And then he was gone, leaving Tilda at the mercy of the cook.

"What's up, Marja?"

Tilda was sure she'd seen the young man who approached the cook before, and frowned, trying to remember. Of course—he'd been down at the docks, unloaded her trunk. What was he called—Stefan?

Marja gave the now stiff egg whites to a passing maid and wiped her hands on her apron. "This lass—what's your name?"

"Tilda."

"Tilda. Well, Tilda's going to help you serve at the welcome tonight."

Serve? At the welcome? Oh, Power! Tilda's heart gave an excited leap. She'd get to see the mages after all—*all* of them. Who'd have thought that coming to help in the kitchen would have given her such an opportunity?

" . . . find her out a uniform, will you, and take her up to the salon when you go." Marja's brow furrowed. "Tralek! Tralek, where's that smoked fish got to?"

"No need to shout," someone yelled. "It's here!"

"Well, it's no good over there, is it? Bring it here, you daft lump," Marja shouted back. Then she looked from Stefan to Tilda and back again. "Well, what are you both waiting for? Go on, get!" She flapped her hands at them. "Get!"

Stefan grabbed Tilda's arm and almost dragged her out of the kitchen into a cooler, quieter corridor.

"You all right?" he asked when she blew out a huge breath.

She shook her head. "No, not really. Everything's happening so fast."

"It does, especially when you're new. Ever done this kind of thing before?"

"No," she admitted. "And I'm not sure how long I'll be doing it, either. Uncle Vanya might find something completely different for me tomorrow."

"*Uncle* Vanya?" Stefan pulled a face. "Well. Better make sure I'm on my best behaviour then, hadn't I? Just in case you decide to tell Uncle Vanya about me."

Tilda's cheeks grew hot. What did he take her for? "I wouldn't ever—"

Stefan cut her short. "Come on, need to find you a uniform. You can't serve wearing that."

Chapter 7

Welcome

TILDA GOT CHANGED in a small broom closet.

"You done yet?" Stefan called through the door. "We need to hurry."

"Almost."

Tilda sighed. There hadn't been time to find a uniform that fitted well; the tunic collar was too tight, and the leggings were too large around her waist. She ran a finger round the collar and stretched her neck, but it still felt as if it were choking her. Then she hitched the leggings up, gritting her teeth when they slipped straight back down onto her hips. Perhaps Aunt Tresa could sort them out later, but for now, she'd have to trust in the Power that they wouldn't fall down while she was serving the mages. A shudder ran through her at the thought.

"Finally!" Stefan pushed himself away from the wall he'd been leaning against when Tilda emerged and looked her up and down. "You'll do." He set off down the corridor.

Tilda held tight to her leggings as she hurried after him through a maze of corridors and up and down steps until eventually, he stopped.

"Right, here we are. The Welcome Room. So called because it's where any newly chosen powermage is officially welcomed to Ring Isle."

Tilda stepped cautiously into the salon, her leather soles squeaking a little on the polished floor. It was smaller than she'd expected, almost cosy. The silver-grey walls had a sheen to them, reflecting the light of what looked like hundreds of candles alight in several floor-standing candelabra and in countless mirror-backed sconces. A large fire blazed in a greystone fireplace, and there were plenty of comfortable chairs and couches positioned close to the warmth. Against the wall opposite the fireplace were a couple of small tables; one had a tray of crystal goblets on it, the other was empty.

"They've done a good job of these." Stefan patted the back of a chair.

"What do you mean?" Tilda ran her hand along the back of a couch, the velvet soft under her fingers.

"Have you noticed they're all blue? They always change the colour on the seating, depending on which region the new mage is going to represent."

"Really?" Now that was something Pa had never told her. And thinking about it, there was something else he'd never told her, either. "How did the regions get their colours?"

Stefan shrugged. "Don't know. They were decided so long ago, I shouldn't think anyone remembers now. Oh, here comes the food."

Two more uniformed staff joined them.

The first man carried a tray, which he set down on the empty table. "Not a bad spread, considering Marja's on half staff," he said.

Tilda stared at the tiny pastries. They were filled with fish in white sauce . . . those dark ones had to beef . . . and was that smoked chicken? There were salad leaves rolled up in flatbreads, bitesized meringue-topped tarts, lemon slices floating in a thick liquid . . . Her mouth watered and she licked her lips.

"'Scuse us." The second man set a crate down almost on Tilda's feet, forcing her to step out of his way. He pulled a bottle from the crate and swiftly uncorked it. "Shall I pour?" He stayed long enough to fill all the glasses with pale pink liquid, then with a quick "good luck," he and his companion left Stefan and Tilda to it.

Tilda leaned over the glasses and sniffed the liquid, trying to work out what the smell reminded her of—something warm and spicy.

Behind her, the door opened again.

"Here they come," Stefan hissed at her. He whipped the tray of food from the table. "You hold the drinks and don't say a word to anyone, understand?"

Carefully, Tilda picked up the remaining tray. Power, it was heavy! How did Stefan make it look so easy? He didn't seem to be struggling with *his* tray. But then he wasn't carrying a dozen glasses, full to their brims, and dainty pastries couldn't weigh very much by comparison. Tilda tightened her grip and glanced towards the door.

Silviu was the first to enter. His trunks must have arrived, because he'd changed into a dark red jacket, a shirt embroidered with little dots of red, and a red cravat, the latter tied in a neat knot at his throat. He made straight for Tilda and Stefan.

"Mmmm, pink ginger wine. Just what I need." He lifted a glass from Tilda's tray. "Vanya's found you a job, then?"

Stefan had told Tilda to keep quiet, but surely it would be ruder to ignore a powermage when they spoke to you? She decided to risk it. "For tonight at least, yes."

"Good." Silviu smiled and moved off to inspect the contents of Stefan's tray. "Right, Stefan, what have you got there to tempt my tastebuds?"

"May I?"

Tilda dragged her attention back to her own duty, and to the person who had taken another glass from her tray. She tried not to stare, but failed.

The lady standing in front of her wore a green dress, its colour graduating from palest green around the neck to darkest emerald at the hem. The bodice glittered with what must've amounted to a small fortune in jewels, twinkling almost as much as the lady's green eyes. A long plait of red hair, threaded through with a few rogue silvers, hung over her right shoulder.

Tilda drew in a sharp breath. Pa's hair had been that colour too, his eyes just as green.

"You must try these, Duska. I think they are pickled lemons from Treytha. They're delicious." Silviu speared a segment of fruit on a thin stick and offered it to the lady.

Duska? Then this was Pergatt's powermage who smiled and took the lemon from Silviu. No wonder she had similar colouring to Pa.

Just before Duska popped the lemon into her mouth, she leaned close to Silviu and whispered something in his ear, making him throw back his head and roar with laughter. He put a hand in the small of Duska's back and gently steered her towards the fireplace.

Tilda's load lightened a fraction more when a gentleman with steel grey hair and a very impressive moustache took not one, but two glasses from her. Tucked under his arm was a walking stick, with a strange, dragon-like creature carved at its top.

She bit back a grin. Like her own tunic, this man's lilac coat also looked to be on the small side, because the buttonholes were straining across his stomach.

"Can you manage them both?"

The concerned speaker had to be the oldest man Tilda had ever set eyes on. His back was bent, his shoulders rounded, and his nut brown skin was covered in a network of fine lines and wrinkles. He was completely bald. By contrast, his eyebrows hung over his eyes like giant, hairy white caterpillars. He looked like a retired merchant, dressed as he was in a drab brown jacket and trousers. But retired merchants did not usually wear shirts the colour of egg yolk with their suits.

The lilac-jacketed man huffed. "Of course I can, Kamen. My limp does not affect how well I can carry a couple of glasses."

Ah, so the older man in the yellow shirt must be the powermage of Kradlock. She should've guessed. Lord Kamen. The other man, the one with the stick, must be the Narganian mage. What was he called?

"Can't manage food as well though," the purple-coated one admitted, casting his eye over Stefan's tray. "Bring that over to the fire, will you?"

"Of course, Lord Taimane." Stefan followed the limping mage over to the couches, closely followed by Kamen.

Tilda stayed where she was, because behind the mages were their stewards. At least, that's what she assumed they were; Uncle Vanya was there in his red coat, and the others wore coats to match. Except for their colours, of course. Kamen's steward in yellow was the only woman; she had a long grey plait and grey eyes that seemed to miss nothing. A tall man with the upright stance and alertness of a soldier wore a green coat for Pergatt. He had a scar down his cheek, and Tilda wondered if he'd got that before or after he became Duska's steward. Last to enter was a short round fellow wearing deep purple, who looked as though he enjoyed his food as much as the mage he served. Each took a glass from Tilda's tray, but only three of the four moved to join their masters and mistress.

Vanya hung back. "How are you getting on?"

"Alright."

So why, now, all of a sudden, did her arms feel so tired? The tray shook and set the remaining glasses rattling, forcing Tilda to tighten her grip even more.

Of course, Vanya noticed. "Put that down on the table before you drop it. But stay there and make sure to pick it up immediately if anyone approaches." He walked away, sipping his wine.

With the tray safe on the table, Tilda flexed her fingers and rolled her shoulders as discreetly as she could, trying to ease the ache in them. She glanced over at the mages and their stewards. She thought she'd been lucky to meet Silviu on her first day on Ring Isle, but to now be in the company of Duska, Taimane and Kamen as well . . . Incredible. And yet . . . She frowned. There were only four mages here. Where was Yaduvir, the new mage of Merjan?

The door crashed open, making her jump. Thank Power she hadn't still been holding the tray—there'd have been pink ginger wine everywhere.

"Sorry I'm late," the man standing in the doorway said.

He didn't sound sorry at all. He strode into the room, followed by a young blonde woman in a blue steward's coat who carried a small wooden box.

Was this Yaduvir? What a strange looking man he was— everything about him looked stretched. He reminded Tilda of the jiraffs she'd seen in Merjan City docks when she was younger, except that Yaduvir's long legs were covered in tight blue and white striped trousers and his body by a close-cut navy jacket, rather than the cream and brown skin of a jiraff. His hair was longer than most men wore it, dark—almost black—and tied at the nape of his scrawny neck with a blue ribbon. His equally dark eyes surveyed the room and everyone in it; when they passed over Tilda, she shivered.

Silviu rose from his seat and stretched a hand out towards him. "Welcome, Yaduvir."

Yaduvir ignored him. "This castle is enormous, isn't it?" he said, walking straight to the fireplace. "I'd have been much later, if Freyda didn't have such a good sense of direction."

Silviu's hand hung for a moment in mid-air, then, with a tight smile, he allowed it to fall to his side. "And welcome to you, too, Freyda."

The blue-coated steward acknowledged the welcome with a slight tilt of her head.

"I hope you found everything that you need in your rooms?" Duska asked.

Tilda strained her ears to catch Freyda's softly spoken reply.

"We have, thank you, my Lady. And I'm certain Ring Isle will soon provide what I lack."

"Good. Yaduvir, will you take some refreshment?" Silviu caught Tilda's eye and beckoned her over. "Pink ginger wine, a personal favourite of mine."

She picked up the tray quickly, heat rising in her cheeks as she walked slowly across to the mages, careful not to spill a single drop.

"I will," Yaduvir said, "but not yet."

Tilda stopped a few steps away. What was she supposed to do now? Go back to the table or stay here until Yaduvir decided he did want something? She caught Stefan's eye and he gave the tiniest of shrugs.

"Wait," he mouthed at her.

"First, allow me to offer the existing powermages a little something to mark their choosing of me." Yaduvir beckoned Freyda forward.

Inside, Tilda groaned. Didn't he realise how heavy this tray was? Why couldn't he take his drink now and give gifts out later?

A frown darkened Silviu's features. "It is the Power which ultimately directs the choice, not we as individuals. It is not necessary to give gifts."

Yaduvir waved away Silviu's protest. "Indulge me." He opened the lid of the box which Freyda held out to him.

Tilda was close enough to glimpse what lay inside. In an instant, she'd forgotten her aching arms; inside the box were four silver bangles, lying on a bed of blue velvet.

Yaduvir picked up one of them. "I have taken the liberty of having these torcs fashioned to match their recipients. I hope they are considered to be well suited." He turned toward Duska and presented her with the first torc, accompanying it with an elaborate bow. "My Lady."

Duska's eyes widened as she inspected what she'd been given. Then she looked up at Silviu. "A mist beetle. On a greenbark leaf."

"A nod to the wonderful forests of Pergatt," Yaduvir said. "I'm afraid that to incorporate any of the marvellous jewels mined in your region fell well outside my budget, so I kept the design simple."

"It's beautiful, thank you. So life-like."

Yaduvir reached into the box a second time. "Now, my Lord Kamen. A skull, to represent the infamous catacombs of Kradlock."

A chill ran down Tilda's spine. The little skull, fixed to the centre of the torc, stared at her with its empty eye sockets. That one was pretty life-like too.

Kamen chuckled as he received it. "You didn't fancy trying to copy the intricacies of the bone stacks, then?"

"The silversmith is an accomplished craftsman, but I fear that would be beyond him. It takes a real master to arrange bones so artfully," Yaduvir replied, dipping into the box again and offering the torc he selected this time to Taimane. "And what else could I have chosen for Nargan, but the head of one."

Taimane grunted and held the torc close to his eyes, peering short-sightedly at it. "Not bad, not bad at all. Looks exactly like the one that nearly took my leg off all those years ago. What did your silversmith do? Shrink it and dip it in molten silver?" He slipped the torc onto his wrist.

Yaduvir reached into the box for the last time. "And finally, for my Lord Silviu. An Ambakian adder."

It was the only one of the four torcs which had been made to look like a complete creature: the head of the snake at one end of the broken band, its tail at the other. Silviu twisted it this way and that until Tilda could have sworn the silver snake was alive and writhing in his hand. Two tiny black stones, embedded in the eye sockets, added to the illusion.

Silviu slipped the torc into his pocket and said nothing.

Yaduvir's lips tightened into a thin smile. He snapped the lid of the box closed and waved Freyda away. "I liked the torcs so much, I had one fashioned for myself at the same time. See?" He drew back the sleeve of his jacket. A silver fish sparkled on his wrist before he tugged the cuff back, hiding it. "I shall take refreshment now." With a swiftness that caught Tilda by surprise, he whipped a glass from her tray and stared at her.

Tilda's own reflection stared back from eyes so dark they were almost black. Just like the ones in Silviu's torc. The glasses on her tray rattled gently.

"Don't drop them, will you?" Yaduvir bared his teeth at her in what he must have intended to be a smile.

It made Tilda think of the animal trophies in Silviu's room. The only difference being, Yaduvir's head was still attached to his body.

"She won't," Silviu said. "Tilda's doing well, considering this is her first day here."

Yaduvir took a sip from his wine, still studying Tilda. "Is that so? New to Ring Isle, just like me, eh, Teeel-da?"

That wasn't how to say her name. The blood rushed into Tilda's cheeks and she opened her mouth to speak. Yaduvir might be a mage, but she was going to tell him how to say it properly, and—

"Thank you, Tilda, Stefan. That will be all," Silviu said quietly.

Tilda swallowed down her words and her anger, and walked back to the table, the nape of her neck prickling all the way. Was Yaduvir still watching her? She risked a glance over her shoulder, but Yaduvir's back was turned towards her now as he listened to something Kamen was telling him.

"What d'you reckon to the new mage then?" Stefan whispered as they both set their trays down.

Tilda rubbed the back of her neck and kept her voice low. "Don't like him. I should think the other stewards are thanking the Power they don't work for him."

A hand reached between them and picked up a glass. "He's not that bad."

For a split second, Tilda saw naked fear on Stefan's face. Could he see the same expression on hers? Slowly, she turned round.

Freyda stood right behind them.

"I-I didn't mean it!" Tilda stammered.

Stefan pointed at the door. "Got to go . . . Get some more . . . tomato crisps," he muttered and walked away quickly, leaving Tilda to face the consequences alone.

She swallowed hard. Oh, she was in trouble now.

Freyda took a sip from her glass. "Don't look so worried. I won't say anything."

"Really?" Relief rushed through Tilda, making her light headed.

"No. He keeps getting a little carried away with the thought of becoming a powermage, isn't doing himself any favours."

The sound of loud laughter made them both look over to where Yaduvir was enjoying some joke or other. A strange expression flickered across Freyda's face, but before Tilda could identify it, it had gone.

Freyda smiled and leaned forward conspiratorially. "If Silviu was right and you're new to Ring Isle like I am, too, we'll have to look out for each other. Help each other along, don't you think?"

"I don't think I'll be much help yet." Tilda nodded towards the group of mages and stewards. "You're better off asking my uncle."

Freyda's brow creased. "Your uncle?"

"Vanya. Silviu's steward."

"How interesting." Freyda took another sip from her glass. "I shall have to talk to him once Yaduvir finally becomes a powermage, find out what my duties entail."

Tilda frowned. "What do you mean? Yaduvir *is* a powermage, isn't he?"

Freyda shook her head. A lock of hair drooped forward and she flicked it out of the way before answering. "He was nominated as a candidate and shortlisted, then the existing mages tapped into the Power to make the final choice. All the others will have been rejected." Her voice hardened and a dangerous glint appeared in her eyes. "Only the best are chosen by the Power, apparently." She downed the rest of her drink in a couple of gulps, her fingers so tight on the stem of the glass, her knuckles turned white.

She'd break the glass if she wasn't careful. Tilda was just about to tell her to take care, when Freyda shook her head and relaxed her grip.

"The initiation," she said. "That's when Yaduvir becomes a true powermage. And I am looking forward very much to the ceremony."

Tilda nodded. "Me too. I'll be able to tell Ma all about it in my—"

"Freyda!"

"Looks like I'm needed. Here, take this." Freyda pushed her empty glass into Tilda's hand and walked away to answer Yaduvir's summons.

Tilda stayed beside the table, but no-one seemed to want anything else to eat or drink, and Stefan hadn't come back either. How long would she have to stand here, doing nothing? She stifled a yawn and looked round for a clock.

Instead, she caught Vanya's eye, and stifled another yawn.

Excusing himself, he walked over. "I don't think you'll be needed any more tonight," he told Tilda. "Leave the trays here and head home. Can you remember the way?"

"Um . . . I think so." And if she couldn't, well, she'd just have to ask someone.

"Good. Tell your aunt I shouldn't be too late." Vanya rested a hand on Tilda's shoulder. "You've done a good job here. Well done."

At the door, Tilda's neck prickled again. She was definitely being watched. Was it Yaduvir? No—when she turned to check, it was Freyda's eye she caught.

But what stuck in Tilda's mind all the way back to Uncle Vanya's rooms, and made her uneasy, was the memory of Yaduvir's black eyes as he'd studied her, and the way he said her name . . .

Chapter 8
The Initiation Robe

IN SPITE OF a promising start and a couple more days serving staff instead of mages, Tilda found that her services were not required permanently by the kitchen.

"I'm sorry, Tilda, but now my folk are all fit and well, I don't need you anymore," Marja told her on the third day.

Uncle Vanya was less than happy when she took the news back to him. "I can't find you something else right now. It's the initiation tomorrow! Have you any idea how much there is still to do? I can't take time out from that to fix you up with something." He looked at Tresa. "Can't she do some of your stitching?"

"I'm not very good with a needle and thread," Tilda admitted.

Vanya huffed. "Maybe it's about time you got some practise in."

"I've a suggestion." Tresa flipped the potato cakes she was frying and pressed them into the pan with a spatula. "If you've got so much still to do to prepare for the initiation, why not let Tilda help you?"

Now that sounded like a much more interesting idea. "Can I? Please?" Tilda begged.

"You are joking?" Vanya stared at Tresa, his disbelief obvious. "I can't simply allow Tilda to undertake the duties of a steward. It's a very responsible position and if she got anything wrong, especially for the initiation, then—"

"Oh, hush, man!" Tresa pointed the spatula at him. "You know as well as I that there are lots of things Tilda could help you with. Like laying out Silviu's clothes or fetching him food because, I swear, that man often forgets to eat when he's about his powermaging business."

She turned back to her cooking. "So. You take Tilda with you this afternoon and tomorrow morning, let her help."

Tilda almost felt sorry for her uncle. Only almost, though. She'd been here for several days and hadn't found out much more about the mages since the welcome. She knew their names and what they looked like, but had found out nothing at all about how they used the Power. Aunt Tresa didn't know it, but with her suggestion, she'd given Tilda another chance to get close to Silviu, right before an initiation. If that didn't teach her something about the Power, well, she didn't know what would. She pressed her hand against her stomach, trying to still the flutter of excitement she could feel there.

Except helping Uncle Vanya didn't work out quite as well as Tilda hoped it would. That afternoon, Vanya sent her to the laundry to fetch a pair of Silviu's trousers. Which would have been fine, had she not lost her way going there and spent a good hour or more wandering the corridors trying to find it, so that there was nothing left to do when she eventually got back to Silviu's rooms. And the following morning, when Uncle Vanya needed to lay out the clothes Silviu had requested for the initiation ceremony, the only thing Tilda had been allowed to lay out on the bed was a plain white shirt. Vanya had done everything else.

Perhaps stitching with Tresa wouldn't have been such a bad choice after all.

"And here's Silviu's initiation robe, which he designed himself," Vanya announced, laying a long, heavy robe beside the shirt and trousers. He smoothed a miniscule crease from the fabric, then wagged a finger at Tilda. "Now, he's asked me to check on something in the Ring Room, and no one apart from the mages or their stewards are permitted to enter that place outside of any ceremony. While I'm doing that, you will stay here until I return. Don't. Touch. Anything."

Tilda heaved a huge sigh once he was out of sight. What was she supposed to do while she waited? Twiddle her thumbs?

She glanced at the bed and the clothes laid there. She'd assumed Silviu's robe would be red like everything else associated with

Ambak, but it wasn't. Uncle Vanya had told her not to touch, but surely he wouldn't mind if she *looked*?

She stepped closer to the bed. "Oh," she breathed.

Embroidered, in exquisite detail onto a heavy white fabric, were colourful pictures. It was the most beautiful stitchery Tilda had ever seen—she doubted even Aunt Tresa could have created something of this standard. The pictures had a backdrop of snow-capped mountains, with lions and tigers prowling on them. Sparkling blue rivers, filled with all kinds of fish, ran down through lush green valleys. And there were towering trees and thick bushes, in which birds perched—in fact, a few were even flying in the clear blue sky above the mountains.

On impulse, Tilda reached out to stroke a grey cat-like creature so life-like, she half-expected it to leap off the material.

"Ahem."

She snatched back her hand as though the grey cat had scratched her. Oh, she'd been told not to touch and she had! Her cheeks burned with guilt and she daren't look up.

"You like the oxala?"

Tilda's head shot up, even as her stomach dropped into her shoes. It was Silviu, not Uncle Vanya, who'd caught her in the act. This was even worse. He'd be even angrier than Vanya that she'd dared to touch something so important, so personal . . .

. . . except he was smiling at her, not frowning.

"He's one of the best animals the robe's creator stitched, but there are more," Silviu said. He took hold of the robe and turned it over to show Tilda the back. "I wanted to include as many of the things about my homeland that I love on my initiation robe as possible."

Tilda leant closer to study the different pictures. "Are all of these real animals?"

Silviu nodded. "Of course. Do you recognise any?" He frowned slightly. "Time's marching on, I must begin to get ready. Has Vanya poured washing water, do you know?"

"I think so."

"Good. Well, take a look at the animals while I wash up. And keep an eye out for the eagle with the wonky wing. He's my favourite." Silviu disappeared behind the screen that curtained off his bathing area.

"Er . . .I can see a bear . . . and a lion . . . lots of birds . . . Oh! I think I've found the eagle!"

Silviu's deep laugh echoed round the bedroom. "He's a beauty isn't he? Not sure whether he ended up that way because of how I drew him, or whether the needlewoman forgot to finish him off."

"He does look a bit battered," Tilda admitted. The outstretched left wing of the otherwise magnificent black eagle was definitely missing a feather or two.

"More realistic though, don't you think? I'm sure there are some tough old birds up in the mountains, still flying high in spite of losing a few feathers."

There were lots of what looked like stunted trees on the back of the robe, all bearing tiny red dots. Could they be berries? Tilda raised her voice above the sound of splashing water. "What are the trees with the red berries called?"

"Bush, Tilda!" Silviu called back. "Ambak berries grow on bushes, not trees. The next time I go home, perhaps you could come with me. Neesha might be glad of the company, she's not much older than you."

"I'd like that."

"Like what?" Vanya said, right in Tilda's ear.

She almost fell over from shock. When had he come back? Had she not heard him because she'd been so caught up in looking at the pictures?

Vanya caught sight of the robe, face down on the bed. "I thought I told you not to touch anything," he snapped.

"I didn't. It was—"

"Don't blame Tilda. It was me who turned the robe over." Silviu emerged shirtless from behind the screen, wiping the last few soap suds from his face. He threw the wet towel at Vanya, who caught it easily.

"That's alright, then." Vanya glared at Tilda and turned away.

Without thinking, she stuck her tongue out at his back.

Silviu chuckled and grabbed his clean shirt from the bed. "Tilda, can you make sure everything's neat and tidy in the other room, while I get changed?"

There wasn't much to do; Tilda pulled a few loose papers into a pile on Silviu's desk, straightened a rug, and plumped up some of the cushions on the couches. She was just wondering whether she ought to dust the animal heads when Silviu spoke behind her.

"Well, how do I look?"

She spun round.

Silviu had changed into the plain white shirt and trousers of such a dark red, they were almost black. Over them, he wore the robe, and as though to show off his complete outfit, he held out his arms and turned slowly in a full circle.

Tilda was speechless. She could have sworn that some of the stitched creatures were moving as Silviu turned. The fish were really swimming, the birds actually flying—she was even sure she'd seen a mountain lion give a silent roar. But that was impossible. Wasn't it?

"Are they—? No, they can't be," she said.

"Tilda, would you like to see the Ring Room?" Silviu asked abruptly, watching her through narrowed eyes.

The place where the Power was drawn up through the Ringstone for the mages to take into themselves?

"Oh, yes please," she gasped.

"My Lord, she can't!"

Silviu sighed. "Vanya, my friend, we are maybe half an hour away from Yaduvir's initiation. Everyone else in the castle will be there and knows what it's like, except Tilda. I'm sure no one will mind if I take her along a few minutes early, just for a look. She'll be on the balcony during the ceremony, the same as everyone else."

Vanya's jaw tightened. "Shall I come now, too?"

"No, you stay here and clear up. Meet us there fifteen minutes before the initiation begins. That should give us plenty of time."

"Very well."

Vanya's voice was heavy with disapproval, but Tilda didn't care. She was going to see the most important place in the whole of Issraya. She only wished Pa could've seen it, too.

Chapter 9
The Ring Room

TILDA FELL INTO step beside Silviu, sneaking glances at the creatures on his robe. They weren't moving now, but she was certain of what she'd seen. Uncle Vanya hadn't said anything about them moving—perhaps he was used to seeing it? And how did you make stitched pictures move, anyway? Surely, Silviu hadn't wasted precious Power to make it happen? That wouldn't be right, using the Power for something so extravagant, simply to entertain.

Pa's face appeared in Tilda's mind, and anger welled up suddenly in her chest, pulling it tight.

"It's been fifteen years since the last initiation," Silviu said, breaking the silence between them. "That was my own ceremony, a year after Duska's."

Tilda forced herself to stay calm and took a deep breath. "Fifteen years?"

"Uh-huh. There were two of us in contention for Ambak, myself and a woman called Luisa. The mages of the time made their decision, aided by the Power, but it was not the one that Luisa wanted." A shadow passed over Silviu's face. "I don't think I've ever seen anyone so angry in my life."

What was it Freyda had said? Tilda tried to remember. "Only the best get selected," or something like that. Which meant that the current mages were supposed to be the best people for the job . . .

"Is it hard?" she asked. "To be a powermage?"

"I can think of easier jobs. It's a huge responsibility to wield the Power on behalf of Ambak. The Power protects us; keeps us from experiencing famine, war, disease—"

"It doesn't!" The words were out of Tilda's mouth before she could stop them.

Silviu stopped walking and faced her. "Oh, but it does. Why do you think the Thoractan Ague only killed your father, when it is a highly infectious and deadly condition?"

Tilda shrugged, blinking back sudden tears. "I don't know." This was exactly what she wanted to find out—but she wasn't sure she could bear the pain that knowing might bring. "I'm not a Medician."

"Neither am I. But I am able to help them."

"How?"

"My fellow mages concentrated on easing Patricio's final hours, but I was delayed in reaching Merjan City. When I arrived, the Chief Medician informed me of a suspected case of Thoractan Ague.

Tilda shivered. Pa—he was talking about Pa, not a "case."

"As Patricio was comfortable by then and my assistance not required, I used what Power I had at my disposal to aid the team of Medicians in containing the ague, That's why, although your father died, no one else did. I protected Issraya. The Power I control cannot be squandered on an individual when the protection of all Issraya is required."

His words hit Tilda like a slap. So the Power would have been considered squandered if it had been used to save Pa, would it? And yet it had been perfectly acceptable to use it to ease Patricio towards his death? What right had the mages to choose one over the other? So what if the ague was infectious and others might have caught it? *Pa died!*

Silviu rested his hand gently on Tilda's shoulder; she shrugged it off, too angry to accept any comfort.

"Tilda," Silviu said gently, "believe me when I say that everything possible was done to help your father. If any of us could have saved him, we would have. Unfortunately, he was too ill, even for the Power."

Anger boiled up inside Tilda. But the Power was . . . powerful! Pa had always told her so. If it was as powerful as he'd always believed, it should have helped him, should have made the mages try harder, worked a miracle . . .

"I *am* sorry, Tilda."

Silence fell heavy between them.

Silviu sighed. "Do you still want to see the Ring Room?"

Tilda nodded, and they continued to walk in silence, deeper and deeper into the castle.

Eventually, Silviu stopped in front of a pair of huge wooden doors painted silvery grey. "Here we are. Come, see."

As soon as Tilda stepped into the room, a wave of dizziness hit her. She stumbled and grabbed the door frame.

Silviu took her arm. "What's wrong?"

"N-n-nothing," Tilda murmured.

Her dizziness was gone almost as quickly as it came, leaving her feeling instead as though she'd been enveloped in a thick, warm, sea mist. It wasn't an uncomfortable sensation . . . it reminded her of being at home, sitting beside the fire, all wrapped up in one of Ma's thick knitted blankets while she listened to another of Pa's stories. She felt . . . safe. Yes, safe.

She pushed herself away from the door and pulled herself upright. "I'm fine."

"You're sure?" Silviu searched her face, looking for . . . what, exactly?

"Yes. Please, can we carry on?"

"Of course." Silviu let go of her arm and pointed above his head as he led her further into the room. "Above us is the balcony, where everyone who isn't a mage or their steward stands during the initiation. It's the only time those not associated closely with the Power are allowed in here."

So why was he bringing her in, now? Was this more evidence of Silviu's willingness to bend the rules around all things Power related?

Tilda moved out of the balcony's shadow, passing between two of the massive stone columns which supported it. Although the room appeared to be circular, the balcony had five definite faces to it, each one sitting atop an arch formed between neighbouring pillars. The balcony itself was painted in the same silver grey of the main doors, but some sort of writing, in gold, ran all the way round the faces. Tilda couldn't make head nor tail of it—it might be any one of a number of languages. Perhaps it was old Issrayan?

A shadow passed over the room, and Tilda looked up, surprised. "There's a hole in the roof," she gasped, as clouds scudded across a circle of bright blue sky where there should have been a ceiling.

Silviu chuckled. "I assure you, there's not. The ceiling is made of glass."

"Oh—the crystal dome on top of the tallest tower?" Tilda rubbed the crick in her neck.

"Fabulous, isn't it? But there's the best bit. The Ringstone." Silviu pointed.

Really? The black stone standing right in the centre of the room was a roughly hewn lump and unpolished, unremarkable. She'd expected something more impressive.

Silviu walked towards it, across a geometric mosaic of purple tiles edged in gold.

Tilda hadn't noticed the colour at her feet; she looked down. She was standing on a large purple triangle, the tip of it behind her, pointing at the centre of the arch through which she'd entered, the base in front, near the Ringstone. To her left was another triangle set into the floor—a red one—and to her right, a yellow. Slowly, she walked a full circle around the room. There were five triangles . . . She started on purple, walked over yellow, green, blue, red . . . and back to purple. Each of them were edged in gold and pointed to a different arch under the balcony. Where their bases touched, near the centre of the room, they formed a pentagon completely filled with golden tiles; the Ringstone stood right in the middle of them.

"It's a star," Tilda murmured. "With one point in each of the region's colours." She looked at Silviu, who was standing on the golden tiles. He beckoned her closer.

Tilda held her breath as she stepped onto the glowing golden floor.

The Ringstone was slightly higher than her waist, and set into its flat polished top were five silver-grey rings—too large to fit on a finger, but maybe not quite wide enough to slide over a wrist—linked to form a circle of circles. There was a faint silvery light, shimmering like heat haze, in the air above them.

"They're made of silviron," Silviu told her. "It's the metal from which stars are made. One fell from the heavens and landed here, in Issraya, millennia ago."

He closed his eyes and touched one of the rings. A coloured light shot up from it; deep red, the colour of Ambak.

Tilda sucked in a breath. "So that's how the regions got their colours."

Silviu's eyes shot open. "What?"

Before she could explain, Tilda heard footsteps behind her.

"Silviu," Vanya called, hurrying towards them. "Yaduvir called by your rooms. I had to tell him you were here, but gave directions for the long way round. I took a few short cuts so I could arrive first, take Tilda away before he got here."

Silviu nodded. "Of course. Thank you, my friend. Tilda, go with your uncle."

She had time for one last glance at the Ringstone before Uncle Vanya took hold of her arm and pulled her towards the door; the silvery haze was back again, leaving no hint of the brilliant red light she was sure she'd seen just moments ago.

Chapter 10
Initiation

IN THE CORRIDOR outside the Ring oom, Vanya pulled a large key from his pocket and unlocked a narrow door, striped in the five regional colours.

"This goes up to the balcony," he told Tilda. "It's only ever unlocked for an initiation ceremony."

Tilda had only managed to climb a few of the stairs behind the door when she heard Yaduvir's voice in the corridor.

" . . . certain there must be a quicker way here. Why didn't you think to find out, Freyda? I was determined to be the first to arrive . . ."

She carried on climbing. Poor Freyda, taking the blame when it was Uncle Vanya who'd sent them on a deliberately roundabout route.

She emerged onto the balcony and looked down into the Ring Room. Below, the star of coloured tiles was much more obvious, the yellow, green, and purple points closest to her vantage point, the red and blue opposite. Silviu was standing perfectly at ease on the red triangle.

Yaduvir, dressed simply in grey trousers and a plain white shirt, had planted himself firmly on the blue tiles, hands on his hips, as though claiming them for his own. His voice carried clearly up to the balcony.

"—wanted to be the first here. It is my initiation, after all."

"I have only just arrived myself." Silviu's voice rose up to the balcony too. "It matters not who is first, because we all need to be present before we can begin the ceremony."

Ha. That told him.

Yaduvir's black eyes slid up to the balcony, and Tilda jerked back, hoping he hadn't seen her.

"I see that Vanya and Teeel-da are already here," she heard Yaduvir say.

Power. He had.

"Vanya is making sure she is settled before he joins me."

"I must go down," Uncle Vanya told Tilda, keeping his voice low. "Will you be alright on your own?"

Of course she would—and she wasn't alone for very long. Soon after Vanya left, the balcony began to fill with other members of the castle staff. Stefan grinned at Tilda from the opposite side, a green kerchief that was very definitely not part of his uniform tied around his throat. In fact, the majority of the staff appeared to have supplemented their uniforms with small items of colour—a bow in their hair, a coloured belt, a ribbon pinned to a jacket—in one of the regions' colours. Tilda wished she'd known. She was trying to think of what she had that was blue that would have done the job— perhaps the blue shell brooch Pa had bought for her last birthday?— when she spied her aunt waving at her from the top of the stairs, a yellow ribbon threaded through the plait pinned over the top of her head.

Tresa jostled her way around the now crowded balcony towards Tilda, using her elbows and boots to speed her passage. "Sorry! Oops, was that your toe? Just coming through . . . yes, thank you! Apologies . . . 'scuse me! If you don't mind . . ." Eventually, she squeezed herself between Tilda and a stout cargoman wearing a purple cravat, and peered over the balcony. "Well. I'm glad to see Vanya put you in a good spot. We'll be able to see Silviu and the new Powermage easily from here, being right opposite Ambak and Merjan."

"Why do we have to watch from up here?" Feeling braver now, Tilda peered over the balcony again. The floor below was empty. Where had Silviu and Yaduvir gone?

She blinked. The silver haze was dancing over the Ringstone again.

"Well, when there's an initiation, there's obviously one mage who's never tapped into the Power before." There was a tremor in Tresa's voice. "Sometimes . . . they don't get the words right. And one wrong word in the chanting can do all sorts of damage to those closest to the Ringstone if the Power can't be contained. We're reasonably safe up here."

Tilda chewed her lip. She hadn't realised the Power could be dangerous. She'd only ever thought of it as being a force for good. "So what happens if—"

"Hush," the cargoman whispered. "They're starting!"

A tense silence fell on the balcony, and Tilda leaned out as far as she dared; she wasn't going to miss a single moment of this ceremony.

The mages emerged from directly underneath her feet. Silviu came first, followed by Duska, Kamen, and then, Taimane. Their short procession circled the Ringstone, much as Tilda had done herself, until they came to a halt on their respective region's colours. They all looked incredible in their initiation robes, and as the stewards entered and took up positions at the pointed ends of the star's arms, Tilda gazed in awe at the different designs.

Kamen's robe appeared stiff and solid, its fabric obviously rough in texture and creased with shadows. There was no real colour to it at all, except shades of granite grey and slate blue and creamy white. Stone. That's what it reminded Tilda of: stone. Hopefully it was much lighter to wear than it looked.

Taimane's coat was deep purple. The Nargan dragon which topped his walking stick had been recreated on the back of the coat in contrasting shades of yellow and gold fabric, its glittering eyes seeming to stare straight at Tilda from between Taimane's shoulder blades.

Duska's robe wasn't really a robe, or a coat. It looked instead like a long cape, fashioned from fabric leaves which cascaded down her back in shades of spring and summer greens at the shoulder, merging into the yellows and oranges, reds and browns of autumn nearer her feet.

At an unseen signal, the mages all walked forward and stepped onto the golden tiles of the pentagon.

Silviu's eyes lifted to the balcony, his gaze passing over the assembled staff. Into the expectant silence, his voice rang out as clear as a bell. "We are gathered today to welcome our new powermage, Yaduvir of Merjan. He is our man of choice and is invited here to be initiated into the mystery of powerbearing."

Yaduvir emerged from the shadow of the balcony nearest to the blue ray of the star and strode confidently forward. He stopped two paces away from the golden pentagon.

"Where's his robe?" Tilda whispered, only to be hushed by Tresa.

The four initiated mages spoke in unison. "Do you, Yaduvir, agree to be used as a vessel for the Power, and swear to use that Power for the good of Issraya in the service of its land and people?"

"I do."

Freyda walked into view and approached her master, a mass of blue fabric draped across her outstretched arms: Yaduvir's initiation robe.

What would his be like? Tilda chewed a thumbnail as she waited impatiently for Freyda to finish helping Yaduvir into it. Freyda finally backed away and a murmur of appreciation rippled around the spectators as they saw the robe properly for the first time.

Tresa let out a low whistle of appreciation. "Whoever stitched that one has a good eye," she murmured.

Tilda had to agree; Yaduvir looked as though he was encased in waves. Panels of different textured fabrics rippled around his body, embellished with glittering thread and tiny sparkling jewels to create the effect of light playing over the surface of water. From the brightest turquoise of a sunny day to the deepest grey of a winter storm, every colour that Tilda had ever seen in the water of the Inland Sea was represented—grey, turquoise, bright blue, green . . . She'd never seen anything like it.

Yaduvir stepped onto the golden tiles; Silviu took one of his hands, Duska the other, and they raised them high.

"Then we welcome you to our fellowship!" the four initiated mages cried.

A great cheer rang out on the balcony, followed by loud applause. Yaduvir's hands were loosed and he smiled, accepting the words of welcome offered by his fellow mages and basking in the attention.

Eventually, Silviu raised a hand to silence the watchers on the balcony, and the applause petered out. "The welcome made, we seek to continue the task set before us. To take into ourselves the Power bestowed on Issraya through the conduit of the rings. Let us proceed." He opened his arms wide, embracing all five mages in the gesture. As one, they reached into the silver haze that still shimmered above the stone

Tilda braced herself. This was it, the moment of transfer. Aunt Tresa had said that sometimes things went wrong, but she hoped desperately that today, everything would go right.

Duska was first to touch a ring; a strand of coloured flame shot up, just like it had for Silviu, but it was green, not red. The other mages followed quickly, until there were five strands of colour writhing above the silviron rings—purple, green, yellow, red, blue— each growing in the intensity and depth of its colour.

"Look at the colours," she whispered to Aunt Tresa.

Tresa frowned. "Colours of what?"

"The li . . . You can't see them?"

"Shhhh!"

Tilda's stomach churned. Surely she wasn't the only one who could see the flames of light? What *were* they? It couldn't be . . . no, surely not . . .

Below her, the mages had begun to chant.

"Hastel athor, embarak nouray. Ilsteth horat umbaroth, clostardith verasta . . ."

Tilda didn't understand what they were saying, but it was like listening to a song, an old song, full of deep meaning. She closed her eyes to listen, letting the words wash over her until there was a change in the rhythm of the chant. It seemed to have more energy, was somehow pulling at her. She opened her eyes.

With a jolt, she saw that the coloured flames were growing, the separate strands snaking up the arm of the mage who represented the region of that colour. She watched, fascinated, noticing that Silviu's red light flowed smoothly, like syrup. Duska's wove a pretty dance, frequently changing direction. Taimane's spiralled around his arm, and Kamen's climbed slowly and steadily. Yaduvir's blue light jerked along a little at a time, almost as though it was having to be coaxed in stages up his arm.

Without warning, a discordant note broke into the chant, and Tilda winced. It did not last long—was gone almost as quickly as it came—and the chanting continued as before. Perhaps the strange sound was a necessary part of the chant, because the mages were now almost completely surrounded by brilliant auras.

Tilda heard the sound again. Several notes this time, joined together in a phrase so at odds with the main chant that it set her teeth on edge. Her stomach churned and she retched. Something felt very wrong.

"What's the matter?" Tresa hissed.

The main chant drowned out the odd sound just long enough for Tilda to take a deep breath and whisper, "The chant, can you hear it?"

"Course I can."

"But the bit that doesn't fit—oh!"

The wrong sounds broke into the chant again, and this time they didn't stop. Was it possible for mere noise to be darkness and threat and hurt? Tilda's bones ached so hard, she could barely stand, had to fight to stay upright and not collapse under the sheer awfulness of it. The sound writhed between the words of the powermages' chant, breaking it and twisting its meaning, building to a crescendo until it almost smothered the original.

With a groan, Tilda slumped against the balcony wall and retched again.

Could no one else hear it? Couldn't anyone see that the auras around the mages were shrinking? Why hadn't anyone noticed the colour creeping back towards the rings? Why wasn't anyone else aware of this terrible sound and what it was doing?

Except it wasn't just a sound . . . not now. There were words, too. And if there were words, someone had to be speaking them. Tilda glanced round the balcony, but everyone standing there was silent as they watched the mages at the Ringstone.

That only left the stewards, or the mages.

A dreadful thought popped into Tilda's head. Aunt Tresa had said the new mage sometimes got it wrong . . . Quickly, she looked at Yaduvir.

His lips were moving, but not to the same pattern as Silviu and Duska, the only other mages facing Tilda. Was it him? Was he getting the words wrong and damaging the chant?

She opened her mouth to shout a warning, but stopped when she heard Silviu's voice raised above the others.

"Extallambeth thrar playthmell, frantathmey strantanth."

These words were somehow protecting, comforting, and full of power. They made the hairs on the back of Tilda's neck stand up on end.

A great surge of energy rippled through the air like a shockwave. Sparks exploded from the obelisk, showering the mages in silver-grey fire.

Duska screamed and spun away from the Ringstone, her connection with it broken. What remained of her green aura flashed violently, then shrank back to the stone, pulsing angrily above one of the rings. Kamen was thrown back even more violently; he landed in a crumpled heap halfway across the room. His steward rushed forward to help, but at a sharp gesture from Silviu, skidded to a halt and left her master stirring feebly where he'd fallen. The yellow light that had surrounded Kamen pulsed in time with the green.

"Power preserve us!" Tresa shrieked. "The invocation's failed! Run!"

Fear spread quickly, and those on the balcony pushed and shoved, making for the stairs.

Tilda's mouth went dry. She gripped the balcony until her knuckles turned white. Run? She couldn't run. Silviu was staring straight up at her, his eyes boring into her like ice blue drills. Was he using Power to keep her here? Dimly, she was aware of Tresa's nails digging into her hands, trying to prise them away.

"Tilda! Please—"

There was one last desperate, failed tug, then Tilda stood alone, watching the last three mages who remained in contact with the Ringstone.

Taimane was fighting hard to keep his hand pressed against his ring, but when silver-grey flames burst out of his sleeve, he yelled and snatched his hand away. Quickly, he shrugged off his robe and stamped the fire out.

A purple light joined the green and yellow, and Tilda's heart pulsed in time with them.

Only Yaduvir and Silviu seemed to be unaffected by the fire. Ignoring the other mages and the stewards standing helpless, the two men continued to chant.

Yaduvir's poisonous words were drawing all the strands of coloured light towards him.

Silviu's body jerked violently, as though reacting to the pull on the red light which still remained in contact with him. "Ustarath un abnarthor!" he growled, and suddenly all of it—the flames of light, the silver fire, the sparks—drew back to the Ringstone and, as though someone had snuffed a candle, winked out.

Tilda experienced a great sucking sensation; for a split second there was no colour, no sound, no life, within the room.

"Grayth althar vrell!" Silviu shouted.

A second explosion of energy ripped through the room. Tilda felt as though someone had punched her in the chest. She tried to suck in a breath, but her lungs wouldn't respond.

Yaduvir dropped senseless to the floor, and Silviu staggered away from the obelisk, barely able to stand.

Tilda stared at the Ringstone, not wanting to believe what her eyes were telling her. There was no silvery haze. No coloured lights.

And worst of all, there were only four silver-grey rings visible in the black stone. Where the fifth should have been, there was empty space.

A terrible sense of loss washed over her.

"The circle's broken!" Duska cried, rushing forward.

"I had to . . ." Silviu's voice was hoarse. He glanced up at the balcony and once again his pale eyes locked onto Tilda's.

There was a moment of horrified silence, then everyone spoke at once.

"But why?"

"What have you done?"

"Silviu, you idiot!"

Tilda still couldn't breathe. The room spun around her. A red mist fell across her eyes, her vision darkened at the edges, and she fell unresisting into the growing darkness.

Chapter 11
Isolation

TILDA OPENED HER eyes. Where was she? This wasn't her room. It was all red, far too red . . . She turned her head on the pillow. A tree-root chair, a desk and bookshelves, instead of the painting of the cobbler's shop. She was in—

"Silviu's room!" She sat up quickly. "Oooh!"

"Steady, steady." A concerned face swam into focus: Aunt Tresa. She pushed Tilda gently back down on the bed. "You've had a shock. Been exposed to raw Power, that's what Silviu said. And there's not many living who can say that who aren't mages."

In a dreadful rush, everything came flooding back. The broken chant, the silver fire, Yaduvir pulling the coloured flames towards him, and—

"The ring! It's gone, we have to do something." Tilda flung her legs over the side of the bed and stood on wobbly legs.

"We don't have to do anything." Tresa took Tilda's elbow, steadying her. "The mages will sort it out."

"But how? There's only four of them left. Yaduvir was trying to take all the colours, but Silviu stopped him and—"

Sheer panic choked off the rest of Tilda's words. Not because of the battle of words and light she'd witnessed, or because she knew that a ring was missing. Not even because she'd experienced that tremendous surge of energy. It was because there was a gaping space in her chest, as though something vital had disappeared. It wasn't her heart; that still beat, hard and fast, against her ribs. No, it was something else making her feel like this. A growing pressure, closing in on her, on the castle, tightening its hold on Ring Isle . . .

The door to the bedroom crashed open.

Silviu, still dressed for the initiation, walked straight over to the window. He sighed and leaned heavily on the windowsill. He didn't seem to realise there was anyone else in the room.

Maybe they should go before he did . . .Tilda tapped Tresa's arm and jerked her thumb towards the door.

"What?" Tresa said.

Silviu spun round. "Flagrantix!" he shouted, throwing his hand out.

A red fireball shot towards Tilda. Instinctively, she ducked.

"Extinguay!"

Something exploded above Tilda's head, but there was no pain, no heat. She looked up. The fireball had disappeared, leaving a faint trail of smoke in the air. Cautiously, she straightened up.

Silviu's hand dropped to his side. He searched Tilda's face, his own expression guarded. "You are not hurt?"

"No." Although she *was* trembling from top to toe. What would've happened if he hadn't realised in time who she was? Would he really have set her on fire?

"Good, good. I'm sorry. I had forgotten you were . . . I would never have—"

There was the distant sound of a door opening.

"Silviu? Are you here?" Duska called from the other room.

Without another word Silviu left the bedroom. "Have you checked the boundaries?" Tilda heard him snap.

"We have. It is as you suspected." That was Duska.

"There's no break at all?"

"None."

Was that Kamen's voice? Tilda pulled Tresa nearer to the door and peeped through. Yes, all the powermages—except Yaduvir—were there, and so were all the stewards.

"Whatever it was that Yaduvir said in that chant," Kamen continued, dropping heavily onto a couch, "it has caused complete and utter isolation of Ring Isle. No-one can set foot on this island, as witnessed by the cargomen when a ship tried to dock earlier, and no-one can leave, as proven by a couple of volunteers who tried. We cannot destroy the barrier that now exists, or even break through it, without sacrificing what little Power we have left in us. And we are going to need pretty much all of that to keep Yaduvir contained."

"Aaargh!" Silviu smashed his fist into his desk once, twice—

"Don't!" Duska stepped forward quickly and caught his arm. He turned on her, snarling, but she held on firmly and showed no sign of letting go. "Silviu . . . The Ambakian ring," she said gently, her face pale. "What did you do?"

Silviu seemed to come to his senses, and Duska released him. The snarl on his face was replaced by a puzzled frown when he looked down at his bruised and bloodied knuckles. "I protected it."

Why protect a ring? Surely it was the people he should've been protecting? A flicker of anger burned deep in Tilda's stomach, but she ignored it and carried on listening. There was still so much she didn't understand about how the mages used the Power. She had to find out why Silviu had done what he did . . .

"Protected it? By breaking the circle and stopping us from being able to draw on the Power?" Kamen shook his head. "I'm not certain that was wise, Silviu."

Silviu flexed his fingers and winced. "I only had influence over Ambak's portion and the one ring. I knew that if I could remove the ring and effectively seal the conduit, then Yaduvir would find it impossible to draw all five strands to himself."

So those strands of colour she'd seen *did* have something to do with the Power. A shiver ran down Tilda's back.

"He came close to succeeding, though." Duska sank onto the couch beside Kamen. "Too close. He might have done anything, anything at all to Issraya." She shuddered.

Silviu nodded. "The words he spoke are strong magic, which I am certain do not have their birthplace here in Issraya. I can only guess at what he was trying to achieve."

Someone started to sob.

"For Power's sake!" Taimane banged his walking stick sharply on the floor. "Get a grip on yourself, Freyda. Crying won't help."

Tilda felt her aunt stiffen beside her, and no wonder; Freyda's head was buried in Uncle Vanya's shoulder. He was patting her rather awkwardly on the back.

Freyda shuddered and lifted her head up. She took a deep breath, visibly trying to compose herself as she wiped red-rimmed eyes on her sleeve.

Silviu drew close to her, his hands balling into fists. "Freyda. What did you know of your master's intentions?"

His tone was so cold, Tilda was surprised it didn't freeze the steward on the spot. She couldn't hear Freyda's mumbled reply.

"Speak up!" Taimane snapped.

"I'm sorry, my Lord." Freyda blinked. "I don't know much. He had several meetings prior to the choosing, and afterwards was excited, hinted of great things to come. I assumed he was speaking of his impending initiation."

"Who did he meet?"

"A woman . . . but he did not name her." She shrugged. "I hadn't known him long enough to feel I could ask."

"You hadn't . . . ?" Silviu frowned. "Why did Yaduvir ask you to be his steward, then? I thought knowing your steward well was the whole point of giving them the job."

Kamen sighed. "Silviu, not everyone has the same relationship with their steward as you and Vanya. My own Maddi was chosen from a pool of applicants only when I knew that I was under consideration. How Freyda came to be employed by Yaduvir is not important at this point. Dealing with the consequences of Yaduvir's—and your—actions however, is."

Silviu inhaled a huge breath and blew it out. "The ring I removed is at least safe for the moment, in my homeland. I have prevented Yaduvir from drawing more Power, but it also means that we four only have available to us what we drew during a failed ceremony. Did anyone manage to recharge completely?" He glanced around those assembled and gave a grunt. "I thought not. We must use what we do have to keep Yaduvir contained and prevent him from accessing the different magic he appears to possess. From what Freyda said, he may have an accomplice, who may or may not also have access to magic. Our only hope is that by isolating Ring Isle, Yaduvir has also cut off this accomplice, but we cannot rely on that." Silviu's expression darkened. "We must assume Issraya is under attack."

Tilda gasped. Who would want to attack Issraya? And why? More importantly, who was going to protect the island, if the mages had barely any Power at their disposal?

Kamen pulled himself with difficulty to his feet. "It is imperative that the missing ring be returned to the Ringstone without delay. We must regenerate the circle, recharge, and defend ourselves. However, if we are isolated—"

"Then we cannot retrieve it, restore our Power, or protect Issraya as we have sworn to do," Taimane interrupted. Two spots of livid colour burned on his cheeks and his moustache bristled alarmingly. "You have made the situation worse by your action, Silviu. You fool."

Silviu's jaw tightened.

"If Yaduvir wasn't talking just about the initiation, but had some other vile plot in mind, what in Power's name do we do?" Duska's eyes were wide.

"I don't know." Silviu sounded exhausted. "We are all battered and bruised, both physically and mentally. Take food, rest, and think on the problem. We will devise a plan tomorrow."

"Then may the Power inspire our thinking." Kamen beckoned Maddi over and leaned heavily on her arm. "I, for one, need to ease my aching bones before I can think straight. Good even to you all."

"I will also take my leave." Taimane shook his head. "Let's hope we can fix this mess, Silviu, because Issraya is unprotected until we do." He stomped out behind Kamen, his own steward hurrying to keep up.

"Take Freyda back, will you, Vanya?" Silviu said.

Hearing that, Tresa pushed past Tilda and joined her husband.

The soldier-steward in green waited for a few moments, but Duska showed no sign of leaving. "My Lady?"

"You go, Isaak. I'll be along soon."

He bowed and took his leave, leaving the two mages alone.

Tilda stood in the doorway and chewed her lip. She ought to go too, but she wanted to apologize to Silviu for doubting him. It sounded as though he *had* acted to protect Issraya at the initiation, even though things hadn't worked out quite the way he'd planned. She wanted to ask him about the coloured lights she'd seen, what she'd felt in the Ring Room, and what any of it had to do with the Power.

Once Duska had gone, that's when she'd talk to Silviu. She drew back into the shadows to wait.

Silviu ran a thumb over his bruised knuckles.

"Let me see," Duska said softly, and took his hand in hers. After a moment or two inspecting Silviu's injuries, she pulled a white handkerchief from her sleeve and bound it round his fingers. "You'll live."

Silviu turned his head away and did not reply.

"You must not blame yourself, do you hear me?" Duska reached for his chin and turned his face back, forcing him to look at her. "You were the only one who realised what was happening—"

No, I did too, Tilda thought.

"—and fought back. The rest of us realised too late to be of any use. If you are at fault, then so are we."

Were there tears in Silviu's eyes? They were certainly glistening.

"I have caused a bad situation to become much, much worse," he said.

Duska smiled. "There will be a solution."

"For the Power's sake, I hope so." Silviu took a deep breath. "You should go, get some rest." He kissed her on the forehead and walked to the window, where he stood looking out over the Inner Sea.

As soon as the door had closed behind Duska, Tilda crept out of her hiding place. She waited by Silviu's desk, shifting her weight from one foot to the other, wondering how to begin.

"What do you want, Tilda?"

Silviu hadn't even turned round. How did he know she was there?

"Um . . . I wanted to ask you . . . about what happened. Before. In the Ring Room. I felt . . . I saw . . ."

"You saw what everyone else saw." There was an edge in Silviu's voice that Tilda had never heard before.

"No, I saw the colours, watched them climb up your arm. And I felt the words, Yaduvir's magic. And yours... I mean, I—"

Finally Silviu turned. He looked at her, a strange, twisted expression on his face. "Go away, Tilda. I have more important things to think about than what you believe you saw or felt."

Hot tears prickled Tilda's eyes. He was sending her away, when all she wanted was to understand. If Silviu wouldn't help her, who would?

"Yes, my Lord," she whispered and closed the door quietly behind her on the way out.

Chapter 12
Silviu's Journal

THAT NIGHT, WHEN Tilda finally managed to sleep, she dreamed . . .

. . . she was scrambling over slick, wet rocks, icy rain stinging her skin, climbing . . . always climbing . . .

. . . a pile of stones, visible through the driving rain . . .

. . . panting . . . her breath short, chest tight . . . tears of frustration mingling with the rain running down her face . . . she had to reach the stones . . .

. . . crawling to the stony pile . . . bone weary, cold, soaked, exhausted . . . exposed . . . alone . . .

. . . the wind drops, the rain stops . . . Silence.

. . . hauling herself to her feet as the clouds fade away . . . sunshine . . .

. . . below, the land laid out like a patchwork . . .

. . . a presence. Behind her.

Turn . . . slowly, so slowly . . . heart pounding . . .

. . . a cloaked and hooded figure . . . its hand stretching towards her, a silviron ring gleaming dully in its palm.

. . . she reaches for it . . .

The hand closes over the ring, flings it away.

And she's watching it travel higher and further than a man's throw could ever send it, towards high snowy mountains in the far distance, where it winks out of sight.

. . . the figure points at her, but she doesn't understand why.

. . . clouds building again, purple like a bruise, filling the sky, lightning flickering deep within . . .

Fear.

Squeezing her stomach, prickling her scalp, running icy fingers along her skin . . .

. . . blue-white light zig-zagging out of the sky, a deafening explosion which blows her off her feet.

Screaming—

Tilda jerked awake, tangled up in sweat-soaked sheets, panting. She tried to pull the dream-images back but they faded away, leaving her with a sense of unease and the light of an approaching dawn, which prevented further sleep. Instead, she tossed and turned until she heard movement in the kitchen. Then she dragged herself out of bed, flung a blanket round her shoulders, and opened her bedroom door.

Tresa glanced up from the stove. "Morning. You not getting dressed today?"

"I'm sick," Tilda lied.

"You don't look sick."

"I feel awful." She dropped into a chair by the table.

Tresa wiped her hands on her apron, then pressed the back of one against Tilda's forehead. "You've no temperature. Did you sleep?"

"A bit. I woke early, couldn't get back to sleep."

"There you are, then. Just tired. Which isn't an illness." Tresa threw three thick slices of bacon into the pan, where they sizzled and spat. "Go and get dressed."

"But—"

"No buts, young lady." Tresa pointed a long fork at Tilda. "Do you think your uncle slept? Or the mages? We're all of us shaken up after yesterday, but if we all took to our beds when some crisis or other occurred, we'd never get anywhere. Power knows there's still plenty of work to do, so you will go and get dressed and we will continue as normal until told otherwise."

Tilda groaned and pulled the blanket tighter. All she wanted to do was curl up and hide, pretend that yesterday—the coloured lights, the surge of energy, the missing ring—had never happened.

"Tilda!"

"I'm going, I'm going." She dragged her feet back into her bedroom and pulled on the grey leggings and black tunic of her uniform.

Breakfast was eaten in near silence. No one seemed to feel much like talking, and conversation was limited to "could you pass the salt?" or "can I have the milk, please?"

Vanya swallowed the last of his porridge, dropped his spoon into the empty bowl with a clatter, and sighed. "We must prepare for difficult times. If we are truly isolated, then no stores can be brought in for the foreseeable future. We will have to ration the foodstuffs."

"We'll manage." Tresa took Vanya's hand and gave it a squeeze. "Even if I have to take a fishing rod out onto the balcony."

"It won't come to that, I'm sure. But I have no idea how the mages are going to get the missing ring back. And if they can't . . ."

"They'll find a way." Tresa rose and stacked the bowls. "We must have faith. The powermages have never yet let Issraya down."

"Hmmm."

There was a knock on the door and Tilda jumped up to answer it.

Stefan was outside, his usual grin missing. "Message from Silviu. He wants Vanya and you as soon as possible to tidy up. He's made a bit of a mess."

Vanya's chair scraped back. "Oh, Power. Thanks, Stefan. Tilda, we leave in five minutes."

Stefan nodded and turned to leave, but Tilda caught his sleeve. "How was he this morning?"

"Silviu?" Stefan pulled his arm away and shrugged. "How are any of us, now we're trapped here with a mad powermage and no Power to stop him? Worried. And scared."

Tilda shut the door. Worried and scared. Yes. That about summed it up.

Stefan hadn't been joking when he said Silviu had made a mess; it looked as though a tornado had ripped through his trophy room. Papers and books were scattered across the floor and over the couches, and a large map of Issraya dangled between two of the animal heads.

Silviu was at his desk, half-hidden by several teetering piles of books. He glanced up as Tilda picked her way carefully around the scattered papers. "You're here. Good."

"You certainly know how to keep a man busy." Vanya shook his head. "Where do we start?"

Silviu had shed his initiation robe but still appeared to be wearing yesterday's clothes. Grey stubble coloured his chin and his hair was a mess, as though he'd been running his fingers through it. Had he been up all night? He yawned, rubbed his hands over his face and then stretched, circling his arms. "A wash, a shave, and a clean shirt. In that order, please, Vanya. Tilda, you can start collecting the papers up. Doesn't matter what order they're in, I'll sort them properly later. Books go back into the bedroom, on the shelves."

At least he didn't seem to mind her being here this morning. Tilda had half-expected to be ordered to leave again. So she set about pulling the papers on the floor into rough piles. They covered a wide range of subjects, judging by their titles: The Basic Use of Power; The Failed Initiation of Grandalla, Mage Elect of Kradlock; A Study of The Dark Magic of Trantak; The Making of a Power Portal . . . At any other time, she might have been tempted to read them, but she didn't want to give Silviu any excuse to send her packing. Perhaps he'd be more willing to listen to her today and explain what she'd experienced? That was more important than finding out how you made a Power portal—whatever that was.

With the floor cleared, it was time to tackle the desk. In between the piles of books were open pots of ink, used paintbrushes, and broken pencils. Tilda set about putting the lids on the pots first. It wouldn't do to spill red or black ink all over the books, would it? They looked old and valuable, the majority of them inches thick, with pages bound in aged and cracked leather. Some of the covers were decorated with unreadable writing similar to what she'd seen painted around the balcony in the Ring Room.

She took several trips to the shelves before it looked as though she had made any impression on the state of the desk.

As she was stacking books for yet another trip to the bookshelf, one of them caught her eye. It was a slimmer book than the rest and had a red leather cover, embossed with five interlocking silver-grey circles.

Tilda traced the pattern of rings. They looked exactly like the ones on the top of the Ringstone—or at least, how they *had* looked. Her fingers crept to the edge of the cover and hooked around it. She had an overwhelming urge to open this book.

No, she musn't.

From the bedroom came the sound of water splashing and the deep rumble of men's voices.

They'd never know, would they? Not if she was quick.

She flipped the book open. Its pages were covered in small neat handwriting, but whose? She turned one page, then another. More writing. Then—a picture. A coloured sketch of a girl with long blonde hair, Silviu's eyes, and a fierce expression.

"Tilda!" Uncle Vanya called from the bedroom.

She jumped and slammed the book shut.

"Silviu says to leave his journal—the red book with the rings on the cover—on the desk. He still needs that."

"Alright," she shouted back, hoping that her guilt couldn't be detected in her voice.

So the red book was a journal, was it? If only she'd had more time to read it. Silviu might have written about the coloured flames and what they were. Or who the girl in the picture was.

Unwilling to risk another peep, Tilda left the journal where it was. There was still a pile of books to take back to the bedroom, she needed to clean those used brushes *and* put these pencils away where they belonged, in the wooden box Silviu kept on his desk for them.

Except when she collected the pencils up and opened the box, there wasn't enough room for them inside. Something unexpected was taking up the space—the snake torc which Yaduvir had given to Silviu.

What was it doing in here? Surely Silviu didn't think so little of the gift, he kept it with his pencils? Pencils, which Tilda couldn't put away until she removed the torc. As she took it out of the box, she shivered. The little stone eyes really were horrible. She shoved the torc into her pocket so she didn't have to look at them and eyed up the last pile of a dozen or so slightly thinner books. She'd stack these on the shelves, then ask Silviu where she should put the silver snake.

"—think I've found a way to leave," Silviu was saying as Tilda entered the bedroom. "There's one thing only to add before it can be used. Then—"

The books Tilda was carrying began to slide. She dug her chin into the one on top of the pile, but it was too late. The middle of the stack slipped out of her grasp and the whole lot crashed to the floor.

"For Power's sake!" Silviu snapped, spinning towards her.

Vanya emerged from behind the washing screen with a shaving brush in one hand and a bowl of soapy water in the other. "Tilda! What are you—"

"I'm sorry, they slipped." She snatched up a couple of the fallen books.

"Leave it. Leave them all." Silviu's eyes had darkened. "And get out."

"Let me pick them up and put them away," Tilda begged, dropping to her knees and pulling the fallen books towards her. "I—"

"Did you not hear me?" Silviu exploded. "Go—now!" He took a step towards her.

Tilda flinched, but Uncle Vanya reached her first. He grabbed her arm and pulled her to her feet, none too gently. "She's going, my Lord."

"I'm sorry, I'm sorry," she repeated as she was hauled out of the bedroom.

Vanya glanced down and his grip eased a little. "I think it's best if you spend the rest of the day with Tresa."

"Is he really so angry with me for dropping his books?" Tilda whispered, blinking back tears as Vanya hurried her towards the door.

Vanya frowned. "No, not really. He's angry at the situation we're all in, and needs to interrogate Yaduvir this morning. It won't be easy. I think the strain of keeping that . . . that . . . man contained is taking its toll."

"Vanya!" Silviu shouted.

"Coming," Vanya yelled over his shoulder. Then he shoved Tilda out of the door. "Go. Help your aunt. I'll see you later." And with that, he slammed the door shut.

Tilda stared at the grey circle painted on the red square. Even Uncle Vanya didn't want her around. Oh, she'd really messed up this morning. When would she next get a chance to ask Silviu where she should put the—

"Oh, Power," Tilda whispered. Slowly she slipped her hand into her pocket. She hadn't . . . had she?

She had; Silviu's torc was still where she'd put it.

What in Power's name should she do now? She could hardly go back in, that would make Silviu even angrier than he already was. But if she kept the torc until he was calmer, he might miss it and, finding Tilda had it, think she'd stolen it. Either way, she would be in even more trouble than she already was. The tears she'd fought to keep at bay spilled over and slid down her cheeks.

Someone took her arm. "Tilda? What's wrong?"

Quickly, Tilda scrubbed her cheeks dry and tried to smile at Freyda. "Nothing."

"You sure?"

"Yes." But she couldn't keep up the lie with Freyda looking at her like that. Her bottom lip trembled. "No. Not really. I made Silviu mad when I dropped the books and he told me to leave, so now I won't hear how he's going to break through the enchantment isolating Ring Isle and I can't put—"

"Whoa, wait—he's what?" Freyda frowned.

A shadow seemed to fall over the corridor. Tilda's eyes flicked towards the lanterns on the walls, but they burned as steadily as they always had.

"Silviu's done what?" Freyda's grip tightened on Tilda's arm and she bent to peer into her face. "Tilda, what do you know?"

"Nothing, really. He just said—ow! You're hurting me!"

Freyda took a deep breath and peeled her fingers away from Tilda's arm. "Sorry. I guess I'm a little on edge. I feel as though I'm being blamed somehow for what Yaduvir's done. If Silviu's found a way past the isolation, then . . ."

"That's good, right?" Tilda rubbed her arm. "I didn't hear how he was going to do it. He said it needed one more thing before it could be used. Then I dropped the books and interrupted him, so I didn't find out any more."

"Hmm." Freyda's eyes glazed over. "A transportation chant . . . or a cleaving throw. Perhaps a thinning force . . . ?"

"What are . . . How do you know about things like that?"

Freyda gave a start and scowled. "I'm a steward. You pick things up when powermages get talking."

"Oh." Tilda had never heard Vanya talk about chants or forces or cleaving throws. Perhaps Yaduvir did more than the initiation chant differently. Tilda shrugged and nodded towards the closed door. "I'm not allowed back in there because of what I did, so . . ."

"Power, if Silviu was mad at you for dropping some books, imagine what he'll be like when he sees me, the woman who stewarded for a rogue powermage." Freyda sighed.

She looked so sad, Tilda reached out and touched her arm. "Silviu's only got one thing more to do. Then he'll be able to leave, find the missing ring, and everything will be alright. You'll see."

Freyda's mouth lifted in a tight smile. "Perhaps. Well, if you're sure you're alright, I will make myself scarce. Perhaps it's best that both of us keep a low profile at the moment." She turned on her heel and walked away.

Tilda shoved her hands deep into her pockets and jumped when she touched cold metal. She still had one little problem to solve . . .

Frowning, she set off in the opposite direction.

Chapter 13

The Red Door

THERE WASN'T A moment during the rest of that day, that Tilda wasn't aware of what she had in her pocket. She couldn't confide in Tresa—she was pretty certain her aunt would tell Uncle Vanya, who'd tell Silviu and . . . She had to get it back, secretly, before Silviu realised it was missing. But how?

She racked her brains for a solution while she unjumbled embroidery threads for Tresa, while she peeled potatoes and carrots, and while she set the table for that night's dinner. But she still couldn't think of anything that would work.

Uncle Vanya returned, grey-faced and silent, to eat. "He's mad," he told Tresa and Tilda. "Completely and utterly mad, is Yaduvir. Everything Silviu asked him, he refused to answer. He just grinned and kept saying 'I've got eyes on you.'"

Those awful black eyes. Tilda couldn't help shuddering.

Tresa shook her head. "How did he ever get chosen in the first place?"

Vanya shrugged. "If he had access to other magic, perhaps the Power didn't have the final say as it should have done. Maybe he *was* able to cast an enchantment over the mages."

Silviu had said as much, hadn't he, the first time he'd spoken about Yaduvir? Tilda had assumed he simply didn't like the man, but what if Silviu had suspected Yaduvir from the start? Why hadn't he kept a closer eye on the new mage, then? Not that it mattered now—Yaduvir *had* been chosen, *had* begun the initiation, and the damage was done. And now, the mages were in trouble.

"How are they?" she asked. "I mean the mages?"

"Not good." Vanya shook his head. "They're keeping Yaduvir confined to one room and blocking any magic he attempts, but I don't know how long they can carry on doing that. You can almost see their Power draining away." He blew out a long breath. "The quicker Silviu can finish what he started, get off this island and recover the ring, the better for all of us."

After dinner, Tilda excused herself. "I'm going to get an early night."

"Goodnight, then," Tresa said. Vanya didn't even look up.

In her room, Tilda blew the candle out and flopped onto her bed. The darkness closed in and she reached into her pocket as she'd done many times over the course of the day. The torc was still there.

What could she do? The best idea she'd had was to wait until the morning, when hopefully she'd be allowed to help Silviu again and could slip the torc back into the pencil box or leave it in his bedroom. But what if he had decided he never wanted to see her again and banned her from his rooms forever? She'd never be able to put the snake back, the longer it would be before it was found to be missing, and the worse it would be for Tilda when it was discovered that she'd had it all along . . .

The solution when it sprang into her head was simple, and made Tilda sit up in bed with a gasp. "I'll go back tonight, when everyone's asleep."

Yes, that would work. Sneak the torc back under the cover of darkness, leave it on the desk, maybe under some papers. She could pretend to find it in the morning . . .

And if she was caught doing it?

She couldn't let that happen.

Tilda lay back down and stared into the darkness for ages before she heard Vanya and Tresa going to bed, and twice as long after that until she heard Aunt Tresa snoring. Only then did she slip from her bed and tiptoe out of the apartment, down the stairs, and into the corridor below.

Moonlight flooded in through the windows, painting the corridor in black and grey stripes. Plenty of light to see—and be seen—by.

But thank Power, the corridor was empty, the castle silent except for the distant sound of waves breaking on rocks.

Tilda set off quickly in the direction of Silviu's rooms. She reached his door and hesitated. Did powermages put enchantments on their doors to stop intruders? She hoped not, but she was about to find out . . .

She reached for the handle, slowly turned it, and pushed the door open a crack.

No bolt of lightning, no sparks, no alarm . . . Breathing a sigh of relief, Tilda squeezed through the narrow gap and pushed the door almost closed behind her.

The room was in complete darkness, apart from Silviu's desk. A small lamp had been left alight there. Its flickering candle cast strange shadows across the walls and animal heads; Tilda could have sworn the various beasts were turning to watch as she crept further into the room.

"Don't be daft," she whispered to herself. "They're stuffed. It's the candlelight, that's all."

This bit of her plan was turning out to be easier than she'd expected. Only a few moments more, and she could leave the torc under a pile of papers . . .

Except there were no papers. The desk was empty, apart from the pencil box and a red book.

Tilda felt sick. No papers? She scanned the room quickly, but there weren't even any on the chairs. What about the pencil box? She flipped its lid open, but it was full of pencils.

No room in the box, no papers to hide the torc under. Tilda rubbed her forehead and tried to think. A drawer—she could put it in a desk drawer. She tried all of them. Locked.

What else could she do? She wasn't going to risk going into the bedroom, and time was ticking away, increasing the chance she'd be discovered and have to explain what she was doing. She'd tried to put things right, but failed. She was going to have to keep the torc, come clean about the mistake tomorrow, and accept the consequences.

As she turned to leave, her eye fell on the red book. Silviu's journal. Of all the books that could have been left out, it had to be that one, didn't it?

Tilda stared at it, and an idea took shape in her head. No one knew she was here. The lamp was lit . . . she was alone . . . why didn't she take another look inside the journal? She could try to find answers to the questions she hadn't been able to ask Silviu directly, find out about the colours and the energy and . . .

Before she could stop herself, the journal was lying open on the desk and she was flicking through the pages of handwritten notes and inked sketches, trying to find the most recent entries.

The last entry was a picture. Of a red door, set in an archway of stone.

Tilda hadn't been on Ring Isle very long, but she couldn't remember seeing a door like that in the Ambakian part of the castle. She'd certainly have noticed that ugly silver gargoyle of a door handle, with its mouth clamped firmly around a large ring. Written underneath the picture was a line of Silviu's neat handwriting, and she read it in a whisper. "The ring lies beyond the door."

The picture shimmered.

What the Power—? Tilda 's heart pounded in her ears. Was it a trick? Some kind of joke? She leant closer to the picture and her stomach flipped over. There was no shimmer now, but there *was* a gap. Between the door and the stone of the archway. Only a small one, but it hadn't been there before she read the line of writing, she was sure of it. The door had definitely been closed.

She ran a finger down the picture, along the edge of the door. It didn't feel like paper . . . it felt like rough wood and flaking paint.

"You're imagining things," Tilda told herself firmly. Had to be. But she didn't really believe it; she knew what she'd felt. She closed her eyes and brushed her finger over the page again, her nerves telling her something that was impossible. She could definitely feel wood, rough and splintered in some places, smooth where it was painted. Then she touched cold metal and opened one eye. Of course, the door handle. She shut her eye again and traced its shape. This was such a clever trick, the door felt so real under her fingertips, could she imagine taking hold of the handle and push the door open?

She could; the door moved under her hand. Tilda smiled and opened her eyes. Then she gasped.

"My hand!"

She could feel it—her fingers were still closed tight around the handle—but she couldn't see it. Everything beyond her wrist had disappeared, as though it had gone through the picture—through the page. She tried to let go of the handle, but it was as if her fingers were glued to the metal.

"Let me go!" She tugged as hard as she could against whatever was holding her captive.

Something pulled back, the sudden jerk pulling her in further.

"No!" Her arm now ended at her elbow. Panic boiled up, acid and hot, in Tilda's stomach and she braced herself against the book, trying to stop any more of herself disappearing.

A third, much harder, tug almost pulled her arm out of its socket and slammed her shoulder into the desk. The impact toppled the lamp and sent it crashing to the floor, plunging Tilda into darkness.

She began to sob. "Please, please, stop! I'm sorry, I—"

"Illuminarka spherus," a man said.

Pure white light flooded the room, blindingly bright.

Was someone there?

"Help me! Please!" Tilda screamed.

The ball of light moved closer; a shadow walked behind it.

"It works," Silviu said.

There was a moment of intense pressure, then Tilda's ears popped and the invisible force gave one last mighty tug.

She had time to scream, once more, as the journal sucked the rest of her in.

Chapter 14
The Girl and the Giant

TILDA LANDED HEAVILY in darkness, in a heap of tangled limbs, the breath knocked out of her.

She heard a loud crash. A flood of light dazzled Tilda as a door flew open, seconds before a huge shape filled the doorway and blocked it out.

"'Ware!" a deep voice yelled.

Before Tilda could react, there was a new pressure on her chest, pinning her to the floor, making it impossible to breathe, darkening her vision . . .

"Abchar. Let her up. Slowly." A second voice. Higher, younger.

The pressure eased, and Tilda sucked in the air she so badly needed. What just happened? Was this another of the journal's tricks?

"Who you?" The deep voice was apparently attached to someone huge, because a very large boot gave Tilda a non-too-gentle, and all-too-real nudge. "Speak, or Abchar make you sorry."

Tilda looked up. The enormous leather boots—and the feet in them—were the anchors to legs as thick as tree trunks. Every inch of the body towering over her—three times the width of any normal Issrayan—was buckled and wrapped and belted in leather and fur. Thick arms were crossed over a barrel of a chest. From her position on the floor, Tilda craned her neck to look even higher. Atop a short, thick neck was a disproportionately small head, with a distinctive ridge of stiff black hair running up and over the skull.

From a scarred face and a great height, a single eye glared back down at her; the other was hidden behind a leather patch.

Acid bile rose in Tilda's throat. "Oh, Power," she muttered weakly. The giant growled.

"Abchar, enough." A much smaller figure, dressed in leggings, stout boots, and a thick fur travelling coat, stepped out from behind him.

Tilda stared at the girl from Silviu's journal.

The girl's eyes narrowed. "That's Ring Isle uniform. Who are you? And how did you get here?"

"I'm T-Tilda . . . I was sucked into the journal," she managed, before her heart gave a frightened leap.

The girl had pulled a knife from her belt. She gave it a menacing little flick. "What?"

"I was sucked into Silviu's journal. I was only trying to put the torc back but I—"

"My father's journal?"

Tilda gasped and scrambled to her feet. "You're Neesha?"

Abchar stepped swiftly in front of the girl, a short sword in each of his oversized hands. "You will not harm her," he roared.

Tilda recoiled. "I never—! I wouldn't—! Please, don't hurt me!"

For the second time, Neesha stepped around the giant and laid a restraining hand on his arm. "She's not a danger, Abchar. Look at her."

Course she wasn't. Tilda shivered and wrapped her arms around herself as Abchar resheathed his swords. She had no idea where she was, but it was cold. "I'm not dangerous, I promise."

Neesha smiled grimly. "We'll be the judge of that. Explain yourself. Properly."

A picture in a book on Ring Isle sucked me in and spat me out here, wherever "here" is.

Oh yes, Neesha and Abhar were certain to believe that story, weren't they? It sounded crazy, even to Tilda, yet it had happened, and here she was. All she could do was tell the truth, however strange it sounded, and hope for the best.

"It started when Pa died," she began.

" . . . I kn-kn-knew Silviu was p-p-p-planning a way of b-b-breaking through Yaduvir's en-en-enchantment so he c-c-could recover the r-r-r-ring, but I th-th-th-think I must've used it b-b-b-y accident. I en-en-ended up here." Tilda's teeth were chattering so much by the time she finished, she could barely speak.

"If what you've told us is the truth, you should be able to answer a simple question," Neesha said slowly. "If you can't, I shall assume your story to be an elaborate lie. You could be working for this Yaduvir yourself—"

"N-n-n-no!"

"So you say. To prove your story, tell me, what is Silviu's favourite creature?" Neesha crossed her arms and waited.

"Wha—?" Tilda's mind went blank. She'd not spent enough time with the mage to know that. Or had she? Power, this cold was seeping into her brain, making it hard to think about anything other than being warm again. She rubbed her arms and tried to think. There were lots of animals in Silviu's trophy room. Was it one of them? She didn't think so . . . Could it be the oxala, because of his fur coat? Or the tiger that had been turned into a rug? Think, Tilda, think!

"You don't know, do you?" Neesha snapped. "Abchar, take her to the berry store. She can stay there until we can get the truth out of her."

"No, please, give me more time!" Tilda put up her hands in a useless attempt to ward off the approaching giant, still trying to push past the freezing fog that was filling her head, preventing her from seeing the answer she was sure she knew.

Abchar grabbed her arm.

And at last, she remembered. "The black eagle! The eagle with the wonky wing on his initiation robe."

Neesha's eyes widened. Then she gave a slight nod.

Abchar released Tilda and she sagged to her knees. She was right, she'd remembered right. Thank Power.

Neesha stepped closer to Tilda and leaned down to look into her face. "You told the truth? Ring Isle and everyone on it has been isolated by an enchantment?"

Tilda nodded.

Neesha slapped Tilda's cheek. "That door was not meant for you," she snarled. "My father's trapped—with no way now of getting the ring back."

"B-b-but," Tilda stammered, staggering to her feet. She pressed a hand to her stinging cheek and blinked back tears. "If it worked for me, won't he come through it too?"

"How much Power do you think he'd have to use to make an enchantment like that? He'll have used so much, he'd be certain to make sure that it could only be used once—by him." Neesha's eyes filled with tears too. "Not by someone like you, a nosy, useless servant."

At long last, Tilda felt warm, but only in her cheeks; a combination of Neesha's slap and a growing sense of guilt. If that painted door in the journal really had been a once-only option, then Silviu had no way to get off Ring Isle. No way of recovering the ring he'd sent away. No way at all to get to the Power he needed to prevent Yaduvir from succeeding . . .

And it was all Tilda's fault. She shivered violently, and a sob caught in her throat.

Neesha glared at her for several long moments, then turned suddenly to Abchar. "Get the stove lit next door."

"For her?"

Neesha nodded.

Abchar stomped away, muttering something foreign under his breath.

"Here." Neesha shrugged off her fur coat. "You'll need this more than me until we warm the place up." She held the coat out.

Tilda took it, slipped her arms into the sleeves and buried her neck deep in the collar. It still held Neesha's warmth, and her shivering eased a little.

"Thank you." She sniffed, and wiped her eyes dry. For the first time, she looked around. The light spilling in through the open door showed she was in a bedroom, the furniture plain and wooden.

The only luxury seemed to be a pile of thick red quilts on the bed. "Where am I?"

"Silviu's bedroom."

Tilda frowned. "But not the one on Ring Isle?"

"No. In our family cabin. On his berry farm. In the Ambakian mountains."

The Ambakian mountains? Tilda's knees turned to jelly. She'd been transported all the way to Ambak from Ring Isle? But that was hundreds of miles, over water and land and . . . No wonder Neesha was angry with her. Silviu must've used nearly all his remaining Power to enchant the picture so it could transport a person so far. A shiver ran down Tilda's spine in spite of the fur coat. Of course he must've meant to make the journey himself. She'd learnt enough about him by now to realise he wouldn't waste Power on anyone else.

Neesha sighed. "Look, it's late and I'm tired. We'd only just arrived when we heard the noise in here and found you crumpled on the floor. You can't go anywhere because of the weather, and Abchar won't let you hurt me, so you can sleep on the couch in there." She jerked her head in the direction of the door. "We'll talk again in the morning."

She led Tilda into a large, sparsely furnished living room. A large lantern, a few lit candles, and the glow of flame from a potbellied stove, which Abchar was tending, gave enough light to show a plain table and four chairs, a cot bed, which filled one entire side of the room, and a couple of sagging couches piled high with animal furs.

Tilda inched closer to the stove—but not too close. She wanted to be warm, yes, but she didn't want to get too near to Abchar.

"You'll sleep there." Neesha pointed at a couch. "What's your name, again?"

"Tilda. Tilda Benjasson."

Neesha picked up the smaller of two rucsacs lying on the floor, slung it over her shoulder, and took one of the candles in its saucer. "Keep your eye on Tilda, Abchar. I'm going to bed."

"Goodnight," Tilda said.

Neesha frowned at her. "There's nothing good about it, thanks to you." Then she opened a door that didn't lead to Silviu's room, stepped through, and kicked it shut behind her.

Tilda tried not to cry. She knew what she'd done. Was fully aware now of what it meant for Silviu, the implications it had for the other mages and everyone on Ring Isle and in the rest of Issraya. Neesha didn't have to remind her.

Abchar stood up, startling her into taking an involuntary step away. It wasn't nice, being the object of attention for only one eye.

"We sleep," Abchar rumbled. With one great puff of air, he blew out the lantern, then blew out the remaining candles too. The enormous cot bed creaked as he lay down and pulled the covers over himself.

With the room lit only by the orange belly of the stove, Tilda made her way cautiously to one of the couches and lay down. "Ow!"

"What?" Abchar growled.

"Nothing, just hit my . . . head."

"Sleep." The bed creaked again as Abchar shifted position.

Tilda hadn't hit her head at all. When she lay down, something had dug painfully into her hip. She had a horrible feeling she knew exactly what it was, and reached into her pocket.

The tiny black eyes of the silver snake were full of accusation as she pulled the torc out into the firelight.

Oh, no, no, nonononono! Not only had she used Silviu's gateway, she'd also brought with her the very object which had got her into this mess to start with. Silviu was going to be so mad. He'd fry her to a crisp for what she'd done.

Tilda curled into a tight little ball around the torc as fear rose up like a wave from her gut, threatening to drown her. What a mess she'd made of things. She shivered again and pulled some of the furs over herself. She was as isolated here as the mages were on Ring Isle. Had no idea where the missing ring was, so couldn't even begin to think about finding it and taking it back—even if she did have the faintest idea of how to get home across hundreds of miles of mountains and forests and fields . . . Tears forced their way through her lashes and trickled down her cheeks. How was she ever going to put all this right?

It was as though she heard Pa's voice then. "Trust the Power, Tilda. Always trust the Power."

He'd always believed it to be real, and she knew it was, now. She'd felt it at the initiation, and had proof of the mages using it to protect Issraya; weren't they keeping Yaduvir and his magic contained, right now? But without access to Power, the mages and the whole of Issraya would be in terrible danger.

It was Tilda in Ambak instead of Silviu. Perhaps it was up to her to act.

Pa's words ran through her head again. She didn't have Power, but she could trust it, just like Pa had. And maybe—just maybe—the Power would help her to find the lost ring and return it?

It was the least she could do to make amends

And in the meantime, she would keep the torc safe until she could return that, too. She couldn't keep it in her pocket—it might fall out. The safest place was probably on her wrist. With trembling fingers, Tilda pushed her hand through the broken circle of silver. It sat too loose on her wrist—she'd have to push it further up her arm. It wedged halfway up her forearm, which was probably a good thing; there'd be no chance of it slipping, and with her sleeve pulled down, no one would even suspect the torc was there.

The silver snake felt strangely warm against her skin and heavier than she'd expected.

Almost as heavy as the weight of responsibility she'd placed on herself to find the lost ring of Ambak.

Chapter 15

The Search Begins

"YOU'LL NEED THESE. It's freezing out."

Tilda jerked awake as a pile of clothes and a pair of boots were dumped on the floor beside her make-shift bed. "W-what?"

"You can change in my room," Neesha added. "Don't touch anything."

"And hurry. Abchar huuungry."

Talk about a rude awakening. One minute Tilda had been dreaming of a silviron ring which was always just a little too far out of her reach, the next she was wide awake and hurrying into Neesha's room to dress. She stripped off her uniform and pulled the borrowed clothes on, struggling with unfamiliar fastenings on the woollen overshirt. Then she pulled on thick leggings, a quilted waistcoat, and three pairs of woollen socks to pad out the knee-high, fur lined boots.

"How long does it take to get dressed?" Neesha yelled from the living room.

"Coming." Tilda pushed her feet into the boots.

"You'll need these too." Neesha, already dressed for the outdoors in a long fur coat, brightly coloured knitted hat and thick boots, threw a coat at Tilda when she walked out of the bedroom. "Abchar couldn't wait any longer, so he's gone ahead. There's a hat in the coat pocket."

Already far too warm in what she was wearing, Tilda slipped on a fur coat of her own and pulled a green and yellow hat she found in one of the pockets over her ears.

Neesha nodded. "Good. Now listen. You are not to tell anyone else about what's happened on Ring Isle. I'll say you're a friend from home and I've brought you up here to see the processing, right?" She ticked off her points on her fingers as she spoke. "We'll talk about it when we get back here, after we've eaten. Understand?"

"Yes." Tilda was perfectly happy to wait a little longer before she explained what she'd decided to do.

"Right. Let's go." Neesha opened a narrow door, and Tilda followed her into a thin corridor which ran along one whole side of the living room.

"Shut the door then, keep the heat in."

There was another narrow door at the far end of the corridor; with every step Tilda took towards it, the temperature dropped. Her breath misted in front of her face, and that white powder on the floor . . . Was it snow?

Then Neesha opened the second door, and a blast of icy air chilled Tilda's cheeks.

Outside, everything was coloured in shades of white and brown. Snow lay piled up against the sides of wooden huts and was packed down in-between where countless feet had walked a path. The air was filled with tiny ice crystals, glittering in weak spring sunshine.

Power, Neesha hadn't lied when she'd said it was freezing. No wonder she'd given Tilda so many layers to put on. Tilda's lungs burned every time she breathed in. She buried her chin deep in her coat collar and stuck her hands deep into her pockets as she slipped and slid after Neesha, who was striding easily ahead of her through the maze of huts.

The path between the huts became part of a large, well-trodden road leading away from the smaller buildings towards a much larger one standing alone in the snow. Smoke rose from wide chimneys at either end of this enormous hut; at least it would be warm in there. Tilda sped up.

Neesha reached the building first and waved Tilda inside. "Leave your coat here."

Tilda shook the powdery ice off the fur and hung her borrowed coat on a free peg. There were hundreds of coats hanging here already. It was like walking into a huge, colourful, furry wardrobe.

"This way." Neesha grabbed Tilda's arm and pulled her through another door into a wall of heat and sound.

As Tilda stumbled behind Neesha towards a large fireplace at one end of the building, she tried to look everywhere at once.

Long benches and tables stretched the length of the room, and filling them were hundreds of men, women, and children. The sound of voices and laughter, combined with the noise of cutlery clattering against crockery, was deafening.

"Grab a couple of bowls and I'll dish up," Neesha said. She picked up a long-handled ladle, secured by a chain to the cauldron hanging on a hook beside the fireplace.

Nearby was a table with a few bowls and spoons on it; Tilda shoved two spoons into her pocket, and held out the bowls. The porridge which Neesha ladled into them smelled of apples and cinnamon, making Tilda's stomach rumble in anticipation.

"There you are!"

Tilda's stomach flipped. It was Silviu, come after her! She spun round, the bowls of porridge held out in front of her like a shield, her mouth open to explain. But it wasn't Silviu hurrying towards her—it was an old man, with a bushy beard, a patchworked waistcoat, and twinkling eyes.

"Bakli!" Neesha's face lit up with a smile and she threw the ladle into the pot.

Bakli pulled her close in a hug. "Oh, but you're a sight for sore eyes," he said, holding her at arm's length. "Somehow I knew you'd be up after the picking." He tweaked Neesha's nose.

She tugged his beard gently. "That's because I'd have to be out in the cold when you're picking, and I'd much rather be warm in the sheds when you're processing."

Bakli laughed. "Thought as much." His eyes fell on Tilda. "Who's this, then?"

"Tilda, a . . . friend from back home," Neesha lied. "I said she could come up with us this time."

"Well, welcome to you, Tilda. I shan't offer to shake your hand as I see they're full, so what do you say to me finding a spare bit of bench so you can eat your porridge before it goes cold?"

"Um, yes. Please," Tilda muttered.

With a bit of coaxing from Bakli, space was found between a couple of giggly young women on one side who welcomed Neesha like a long-lost friend, and a rotund gentleman on the other who talked to Bakli about mysterious things like shaker plates and berry forks and other things that Tilda had never heard of. She kept her head down, concentrated on her breakfast, and looked up only when she'd scraped her bowl completely clean.

Seeing that she'd finished, Bakli elbowed Tilda gently and struck a match on the table. "Watch," he murmured through his beard, using a packed but unlit pipe to point. "Over there."

She looked to where he'd indicated. "Oh, you mean Abchar?"

Bakli nodded and lit the tobacco. "The gentle giant."

Gentle? Abchar? Tilda doubted that very much. But wherever Abchar walked between the tables, he seemed to attract the younger children; they slid off their benches and tiptoed after him. One little girl—braver than the rest, who barely came as high as Abchar's knee—crept out in front of her friends and suddenly launched herself at his legs with a delighted shriek. The rest of the children seemed to take that as a signal and threw themselves at Abchar too, until he was covered in squealing children. Heads turned when he growled and sent some of his assailants running, but the adults laughed and the children soon came back for more, which this time included being tickled when they got within reach of Abchar's long arms.

Maybe he did have a softer side, after all.

"There are a lot of children," Tilda said.

"There are." Bakli pulled several times on his pipe to get the tobacco glowing.

An awful thought occurred to Tilda. She'd seen the children back in Merjan who were forced to clean chimneys or gut fish or sweep shop floors. Pa had hated to see them work so hard at such an early age. "They don't have to *work* here, do they?"

Bakli drew on his pipe again and blew a perfect smoke ring. "They do. But," he said, as Tilda opened her mouth to protest, "best I explain."

Tilda crossed her arms. Children shouldn't work. That's why the Academies tried to insist on an age limit. Was there an Academy of Berry Farmers? If so, she'd never heard of it. Perhaps there should be one . . .

"It's a way of life, berry farming. I was born into it, and I'm now foreman of the place," Bakli said, with more than a hint of pride in his voice. "In the summer months, everyone's back down in the valleys, living in their villages and tending their vegetable plots or looking after their sheep and cows. But round about late autumn, things change. A few stay behind to look after the animals, but most of the families start climbing up here. They have to get to us before the first snow cuts off the roads and they lose their chance to earn money for the next twelve months. The families arrive, settle into their huts— same ones every year—and the single men and unmarried women take a bed in separate dorms. Mind you, there's sometimes been a marriage and a new hut to be built afore the winter's out!" His eyes twinkled.

"So the children come with their parents and are forced to work?"

"Not forced. We're not monsters. They stay inside with their mammas, playing and schooling, while the men go out and pick berries. Tis too cold for the littlies, as the berries need frost, see, to ripen."

Playing and schooling. That didn't sound so bad.

"But during the worst of the winter months, when we're processing, they . . . help out."

"Work, you mean."

"Well . . ." Bakli pulled on his pipe again. "Littlies see it all as a huge game, but they grow up knowing the berries—it gets in their blood. Tell you what, why don't I show you round this morning? You'll be able to see what I mean and decide for yourself if it's work or play."

"Sorry, Bakli, it'll have to be this afternoon," Neesha chipped in. "We arrived so late last night, we still need to unpack. Perhaps after lunch?"

"Fair enough." Bakli craned his neck, as though looking for someone. "Ladil!"

A tall, skinny youth sitting on the next table answered him.

"Remind me to take my lunch on time today," Bakli called to him. "I've got a tour to give after it." The young man saluted and Bakli levered himself up and stepped over the bench. "I must be off, get these folk working. No rest for the foreman. See you later, girls."

It was as though the whole room had been waiting for Bakli to stand up, because suddenly everyone was on the move, stepping over the benches or sliding along to their ends, all jostling each other and heading towards the cloakroom.

Neesha seemed in no hurry to move. She stayed on the bench, playing with a silver pendant hanging on a chain around her neck; the gesture caught and held Tilda's attention. Especially when a faint red glow seeped from between Neesha's fingers. It was just like–

"Right, let's go." Neesha tucked the pendant away and stood up.

Back in Silviu's hut, Neesha indicated that Tilda should sit at the table, and took a seat opposite.

Tilda shifted uncomfortably in her seat, wondering what to say while Abchar fed more wood into the stove. When she couldn't bear the silence in the room any longer, she spoke. So did Neesha.

"We've got to find—"

"I'm going to—"

They both stopped and Tilda's cheeks grew warm. "You first."

Neesha leaned forward. "I've been thinking about everything you told us last night. I've decided to leave you here with Bakli, and I'll find the ring for my father."

"Oh." Tilda blinked. But that's what she had planned to do—find the ring.

"And how you do that?" Abchar asked, knees cracking as he stood up. "You know where ring is?"

"No, but I'm sure Pa won't have hidden it very far away if he made the doorway open here. It's probably in our hut." Neesha jumped up, as though she would search for it there and then.

Tilda chewed her fingernail. Something about that idea didn't feel right. And suddenly she remembered what she'd dreamed after the initiation—a silviron ring, thrown upwards and outwards towards snow topped mountains, not a wooden hut—and heard again what Silviu had said. "The ring I removed is at least safe for the moment, in my homeland."

Hiding the ring here was too obvious. Yes, Silviu could have got it back quickly, but what if someone else—Yaduvir—had come through the door instead?

Tilda shook her head. "I don't think he'd have made it that easy."

Neesha slapped her hands on the table and leaned towards Tilda, glaring at her with eyes so like Silviu's, it was unnerving. "Are you saying you know my father better than I do?"

"No!" Tilda had to admit she didn't think she knew Silviu at all. There was so much he'd done that confused her . . . But there was a sense, deep down in her gut, that she was right in what she thought, and Neesha was wrong. She bit her lip. Was this the Power guiding her?

"Well, if you think you know better, you can just sit there while I find the ring." Neesha stomped into Silviu's bedroom.

Abchar shook his head, sighed, and sat on his enormous bed, head in hands.

Tilda stayed where she was. She ought to offer to help, but why waste time on a fruitless search? She could use the time instead to think about where else in Ambak the ring might be.

Neesha didn't look at anyone when she stormed out of Silviu's bedroom and went into her own.

She didn't find anything in there, or in the living room, but Tilda had to give Neesha credit for persisting. There wasn't a nook or cranny in the hut which escaped her inspection.

Eventually though, Neesha stopped hunting and sat back at the table. "It's not here," she said, in a small voice.

"No." Tilda bit back the "I told you so" which sprang to her lips. "You need to look somewhere else in Ambak."

"Somewhere else in Ambak. Ha!" Neesha got up, and walked into Silviu's room for the second time. She came back carrying a roll of parchment, which she unrolled on the table, right under Tilda's nose.

It was a map of Issraya.

"You do know how big Ambak is, don't you?" Neesha's words dripped with sarcasm. "And how long it would take to search this entire region? Where do you suggest looking then, Miss Know-it-all?"

Tilda stared at the lines marking out the different regions. Neesha was right—Ambak was huge. And a long, long way from Ring Isle, with its five tiny, interlinked grey rings drawn beside it. How she wished she'd never left. She didn't want to be here, looking for a ring . . . but she didn't want to think of the mages struggling with Yaduvir, either. Or of everyone in Issraya being in danger. She'd made up her mind to help, and help she would. "I don't know exactly—"

"Ha!"

Heat rose in Tilda's cheeks. She might not know exactly where—yet—but she trusted the Power to guide her there. She took a deep breath. "I said *I* don't know, but surely we can work it out? Silviu must have made the gateway come here for a reason. Did he know you'd be here, so you'd be able to help him?"

"No," Neesha said slowly. "I only decided to come up two days ago."

"Then perhaps it was the berry farm he needed, not his hut?"

"Hmm." Neesha looked thoughtful. "The first thing Pa always does when he arrives at the farm in winter is an inspection of the processing plant." She nodded slowly. "You might have something there."

"Silviu know every inch of farm," Abchar growled. "Could go anywhere without bother. Others," his eye swivelled to look at Tilda, "can't."

"But I can." Tilda realised suddenly. "Remember what Bakli said at breakfast? He offered to take me on a tour of the farm . . . We could look for the ring while we go round."

Neesha's eyebrows shot up. "We?"

"Well, yes... me and Abchar can look too. Then there'll be three pairs of . . . um . . . two and a half . . . um . . . You know what I mean," Tilda finished, her cheeks burning.

Neesha's eyes narrowed. "Abchar would be too obvious, but with the two of us . . . Yes. Alright."

Tilda grinned, pleased that her suggestion had been accepted.

"Don't know what you're grinning for," Neesha snapped. "Just because we're going to both be looking for the ring doesn't mean I've forgotten it's you who put us in this position. You're going to have to do a lot of explaining when you next see my father."

Tilda wiped the grin off her face and felt for the hardness of Silviu's torc under her sleeve. Yes, she did have an awful lot of explaining to do. More than Neesha realised.

Chapter 16
Berry Farm

LUNCH WAS A thick and hearty potato and ham soup, served with chunks of brown bread still warm from the ovens and lathered in butter. When they had eaten their fill, Neesha sought out Bakli, Tilda trailing in her wake.

"There he is. Bakli! You promised to show Tilda the farm," Neesha called. "I'm going to come along too, if that's alright?"

Bakli's eyebrows rose. "Thought you knew about everything already?"

Neesha shrugged. "Tilda's my guest. I shall accompany her. And things might have changed since I was last here."

"That they might have. Fair enough, then."

Without further discussion, Bakli led the way to one of several large sheds behind, and a short walk away from, the dining hut.

"Keep your eyes peeled," Neesha whispered to Tilda as they followed. "Do you know what you're looking for?"

"A silviron ring, about this big." Tilda made a circle with her hands.

"Good. Just don't make it too obvious you're searching for something. We don't want Bakli asking awkward questions."

With every step she took closer to the shed, Tilda's stomach tied itself into a tighter knot. Yes, she knew what the ring looked like. But what if someone else had already found it? Surely, something like that, appearing out of nowhere—like she had, in Silviu's hut—would have been noticed? What if it *was* here, but they missed it during the tour? Or, even worse, what if it wasn't here at all?

"One step at a time," she murmured. "Trust the Power."

Neesha flashed her a look. "What did you say?"

"Nothing."

Bakli opened a small person-sized door cut into a pair of double doors large enough to drive a cart through. "This here's the berry store," he announced.

Tilda stepped inside and paused to allow her eyes to adjust in the gloom; the shed was poorly lit by a line of small skylights punched into its roof. "Where are the berries?"

"Over here." Bakli walked towards a couple of wide, shallow baskets at the far end of the shed. "If you'd been in here when we'd finished picking, it would've been full to bursting." He plunged a hand into one of the baskets, pulled out a fistful of scarlet berries, and let them run through his fingers. "The shed would normally have been empty by now, but there's still a few parsaweight left to process."

Neesha frowned. "Why's it taken so long? Doesn't usually."

"We almost doubled our yield this year, thanks to the new variety Silviu asked me to plant," Bakli told her. "This way."

"You go on," Neesha muttered to Tilda. "I'll have a quick look in these baskets and catch you up."

"I don't think it'll be here," Tilda whispered back. "If Silviu knows this shed's usually empty by now, surely he wouldn't expect there to be any baskets here to hide the ring in?"

"Are you two coming?" Bakli called.

"On our way." Tilda surprised herself—and Neesha, judging by her startled expression—by grabbing Neesha's hand and tugging her towards the open doorway where Bakli was waiting for them.

Neesha pulled her hand away sharply. "I hope you're right."

A short walk across a yard, and Tilda was ushered into another shed.

"This is the washing shed," Bakli explained, pointing to the wide shallow basins lined up along the length of one wall. "Berries are put in the pans last thing at night. They're washed, then spread out on these tables overnight to dry." He indicated the finely meshed tabletops opposite each of the pans. "The last lot'll be washed tonight, before dinner. We'll come back later so you can see it happening."

Apart from the empty pans and tables, the only other equipment visible was a rack of long-handled nets clipped to the wall within easy reach of the pans.

Tilda looked round, dismayed. There was no ring here—it would have been obvious in one of the pans or on the mesh tables. And the only other place would have been in one of the nets, but they were all disappointingly empty.

In the next shed Bakli took them to, she didn't know whether to be pleased or not; there were plenty of places to hide the ring, but so many people, it was unlikely to have remained undiscovered for long. The room was full of circular tables, seating six women at each. Beside each woman was a tall basket, filled to varying levels with berries. And, Tilda noted with a start, there were children here, too. She frowned.

Bakli beckoned her over to one of the tables. "Come, watch them destalking. Hanna will show you."

The woman called Hanna smiled and picked a fresh clump of berries out of the basket by her knee. She ran a three-tined fork swiftly along the length of the stem, separating the fruit from the stalk. The loose berries ran towards a hole in the centre of the gently sloping table and dropped into another basket positioned underneath.

"D'you fancy having a go, dearie? Tis easy, honest." Hanna offered Tilda her fork. "Even the childer manage to do it when we let them, don't you, Rosa?"

Tilda took the proffered fork and looked down at a little girl who was staring up at her with wide eyes. "When you let them?"

"Aye. Only when they've been good and let their mammas work hard." Bakli ruffled the girl's hair. "And I bet you've been a poppet today, ain't you, Rosa?"

"I bin ver' good." Rosa grinned a gap-toothed grin up at him. "My turn next, Mr Bakli?"

"Your turn next," Hanna said, kissing the top of Rosa's head. She picked a bunch of scarlet berries out of the basket and handed them to Tilda.

It was harder than it looked. Tilda was glad to hand back the fork when her heavy-handed attempts at destalking left most of the berries squashed beyond recognition.

"My turn!" Rosa climbed onto Hanna's knee and seized the fork eagerly. Her deft little fingers stripped her berries without so much of a bruise.

"See?" Bakli murmured. "'Tis but a game to the littlies at this age. Sizing shed's next."

They left Neesha chatting at another table. It looked as though she was doing some destalking too; Tilda felt a twinge of envy when she saw that none of Neesha's berries were damaged. Mind you, if you didn't squash any berries, then you couldn't lick their rich juice off your hands afterwards . . . Which is exactly what Tilda did as Bakli led her to the next building, which was more of a tower than a shed.

Inside, a latticework of wooden walkways and ladders rose up from the floor to almost the height of the ceiling, far above Tilda's head. It was almost like being in the Ring Room, except there was no glass dome. And no Ringstone. Instead, there was a central column built of horizontal metal plates, each separated by a distance roughly equal to the height of two men. A little below the level of each plate were two platforms, built on opposite sides of the column.

"This is the sizing stack, my own invention," Bakli told her. "It saves hours of sorting time. Look—see? There's a basket ready to go." He pointed to a basket, tied to one end of a rope wound around a series of winches and pulleys. A well-muscled man hauled several times on the free end of the rope, sending the basket swaying up towards the roof. The men standing on the uppermost walkway seized the basket and tipped its contents onto the first metal plate.

"Each plate's punched with different sized holes, largest up top and smallest at the bottom," Bakli explained, as Tilda watched the first plate being shaken from side to side by the men standing on the platform just below it. There was a shout, the top plate stopped moving, and the men swarmed down the ladders to the next level. Another shout, and they began to push and pull the second plate.

"So . . . the berries that are too big to get through are held back each time?"

"Exactly." Bakli beamed at Tilda through his beard. "We stop the biggest ones first and gradually the berries pass through until only the littlest ones are left. I've had to add two extra plates this year, 'cause the berries were so big off the new plants. They jammed the works."

If the ring were anywhere in here, it was likely to get stuck on one of the plates.

"What happens if there's something that's not a berry in one of the baskets?" Tilda asked, allowing herself to feel hopeful.

"Why? You've not lost anything have you?" Bakli looked worried. "We have to throw all the fruit away if a foreign object taints it."

"No, no, I just wondered."

"Well, everything gets stuck somewhere in the sieves, because there'll be a point where the holes are too small for it to go through, just like the berries. My men would remove whatever it was and try to find out where it came from to prevent it from happening again."

"No hope of finding anything in here before someone else, then," a voice whispered in Tilda's ear, making her jump. Neesha had caught them up.

It took the rest of the afternoon to see everything that Bakli wanted to show them. In the drying sheds, Tilda sweated in the underground firepits, whose glowing embers heated the air circulating into the room above, slowly drying the berries spread out on the floor until they were shrivelled and brown. She tried Ambak berry jam on hunks of fresh bread, and helped to screw the lids on jars filled to the brim with berries swimming in thick sugar syrup.

She saw no sign of a silviron ring.

The juicing room looked like fun, and Tilda itched to kick off her shoes and join the young women who, with skirts hitched high above their knees, were treading the fruit in vast oaken barrels. "Can I have a go?"

Neesha sniggered. "Well, you could, but you might end up with more than you bargained for."

"I don't understand." Tilda frowned.

"It's a job reserved for unmarried girls. Tis the first thing a young man looks for in a future wife—her ruby slippers," Bakli said, pointing to the juice-stained ankles and feet stamping merrily on the pulpy mess. "They fair dance the juice out of the berries, these maidens."

"Oh." Tilda's cheeks grew hot. Were they as red now as the girls' feet? She ducked her head to hide them. "Can we move on?"

The next shed was much smaller than any they'd previously visited, its walls still weeping sticky resin and giving off the scent of freshly sawn timber.

"This is new." Neesha looked at Bakli in surprise. "What happens in here?"

Bakli opened the door and waved her inside.

The air within was heady with fumes and bright with light reflected from rows of glittering glass bottles. A young man sat at a high workbench, carefully pouring a thick clear liquid through a funnel into bottles already a quarter full of berries and what looked like brown sugar.

Bakli slapped a hand onto the young man's shoulder. "Ladil has come up with a new idea for using up the excess of berries. Would you like to try it?"

Ladil grinned at his visitors. He hopped off the stool and selected a bottle from the top shelf of a huge rack set against one wall. The liquid in these racked bottles was no longer clear; its colour ranged from palest pink on the bottom shelves to deep scarlet nearer the top. A couple of younger children watched with interest as they continued to methodically rotate the bottles on the lower shelves.

Ladil took three thimble-sized glasses from a shelf and poured a miniscule measure of the startlingly red drink into each, handed them out to his guests, and waited.

Bakli tossed his drink into his mouth immediately, swallowing it in one gulp. "Good stuff. Warming," he said, smacking his lips.

Ladil turned to the girls. "Try it," he urged.

Tilda looked at Neesha, uncertain. Neesha pulled a face, and by unspoken agreement they lifted their glasses to their lips at the same time.

Tilda's large gulp made her cough and choke, which set Ladil and Bakli laughing. Neesha wrinkled her nose, took the tiniest of sips, and set the glass down quickly, refusing to drink any more. Tilda waited until her spluttering had stopped, then took a second, more cautious sip of the fiery drink. This time, a pleasant warmth stole through her chest and made her fingers tingle. "I like it. What is it?"

"Ladil calls it 'Bloodboil', don't you?" Bakli chuckled.

Ladil nodded. "Aye, 'cos it gets your insides all heated up."

"It does that." Tilda grinned back at him.

"It'll soon be time for dinner," Bakli said. He finished off what was left of Neesha's drink. "Let's head back to the washing sheds, shall we?"

As they retraced their steps through the farm, Tilda felt distinctly lightheaded and couldn't help smiling.

"Don't know what you're looking so cheerful about," Neesha snapped, keeping her voice low so Bakli could not hear. "It's not like we've found what we were looking for."

"I know." Tilda tried to squash the giggle that rose in her throat. "I think it's Ladil's Bloodboil."

"Huh!" Neesha threw her a look of disgust.

Tilda forced herself to look serious and followed Bakli into the washing shed.

What a different place it was now. All the pans were full of water and berries, the latter floating like a lumpy scarlet scum. Two or three men were stationed by each pan, stirring up the watery, berry-laden mess with their bare hands.

If the ring was hidden anywhere in there, Tilda would have to get involved. "Can I help?" she asked one of the men.

"O'course. Get stuck in!" came the cheerful reply.

She didn't need to be told twice. She rolled up her sleeves, remembering just in time to keep the torc hidden, and plunged her hands into the nearest pan. She gasped at the shock. "Oooh! That's cold!"

"Well, we can hardly boil the berries right at the start now, can we?" A second man rolled his eyes at her, but grinned to show he was making fun.

It wasn't long before Tilda's fingers began to ache, tingling in their tips as though she had pins and needles. How did the men do this every day in the depths of winter? Did they not suffer from chilblains? She wasn't going to let it beat her though; she gritted her teeth and swirled the berries, determined to carry on as long as she could.

Then she saw the red haze.

She blinked, her hands falling still in the freezing water.

"Keep stirring," one of the men said.

Tilda made a half-hearted attempt at swirling the water and berries again; the red haze moved lazily above both.

Don't be stupid, a little voice said in her head. It's the Bloodboil, making you see things.

Except deep inside, she knew it wasn't. She'd seen this haze before...

Slowly, hardly breathing for fear it would disappear, Tilda lifted her hands out of the water, her heart knocking madly against her ribs.

"Had enough already?" another worker chuckled, shaking his head.

Ignoring him, Tilda left the pan and wandered the length of the shed. Now she knew what she was looking for, she could see the red haze shimmering above every single pan.

The men unhooked their long-handled nets from the wall. With practised movements, they skimmed the berries from the pans and transferred them to the mesh tables, spreading them out. The haze was transferred too—but as Tilda watched, it faded and disappeared. Where had it gone? She glanced back at the nearest pan, empty now of berries but still full of water. The red haze was thick above it.

Moving like a sleepwalker, Tilda walked over to the pan and stared down into the water. Her confused and red-tinted reflection stared back.

"Tilda, are you alright?" Neesha sounded worried.

"I . . . Can you see any colour in this water?" Tilda whispered.

Neesha pulled a face. "Colour? What colour? Water has no colour."

Once again, she seemed to be the only one who could see it. Tilda dipped her hand into the pan. The water didn't feel as cold now, yet her fingers still tingled. She pulled her hand out, and saw that every drop of liquid dripping from her fingertips flashed ruby red.

"Happy now you've seen everything?"

"What?" Tilda stopped watching the drips and looked up at Bakli.

"Are you happy now you've seen everything," he repeated, a slight frown creasing his brow.

"Yes, yes . . ." Tilda's mind began to whirl. What exactly was it she was seeing? She'd seen red haze around Silviu and around Neesha's pendant. She had seen coloured flames in all the region's colours at the Ringstone, watched it climb up the mages' arms… Was this… Power? Was she actually seeing Power? If it was, then of course she might have expected to see it around Silviu, but how did it get to be in jewellery or water? And what use could that knowledge be in the hunt for the lost ring?

Bakli's voice seemed to reach her from a long way away. "You ready for some dinner?"

Neesha's reply sounded equally distant. "Definitely. I'm starving!"

Tilda dipped her hand into the water once more and bit her lip when a second shower of ruby-tinted droplets fell back into the pan.

Chapter 17

A Breakthrough

TILDA COULDN'T EAT. She stared at her plate, but didn't see the lamb gravy congealing on her plate. All she *could* see was the red haze, floating above the washing pans.

"What's up with you?" Neesha said. "You've hardly said a word all evening."

Tilda jumped. She'd almost forgotten there were other people in the dining hut.

Neesha sat opposite. She'd pulled her pendant out of her shirt and was running the silver disc along the chain, left to right, left to right.

Even in the lamplight, Tilda could see the faint red glow. "Did your father give you that necklace?"

Neesha stopped sliding the pendant. "Yes. He told me to wear it always, so I'd be able to feel him close when he's away." Her hand tightened around the pendant. "I think he just said that to make me feel better about him not being here. Which it does, most of the time. Though I'd rather be with him. He said there was Power in it, that it would help protect me . . ."

And there it was, the confirmation Tilda had been looking for. Everything suddenly made sense.

"It's Power!"

Neesha frowned. "What? Yes, I just said, there's supposed to be Power in it."

"I know, I . . ." Tilda tried to find the words she needed to explain. "The Power makes a glow around an object," she said, slowly. "An . . . aura."

Neesha shrugged. "So? Pa told me about that years ago. It's something only the powermages can see."

Tilda gasped. "But *I* can see it!"

"You can't!" Neesha jumped up, her face fierce.

Tilda's insides froze. Was this something else she'd done wrong without meaning to? She couldn't help what she could see… And she *could* see Power, was certain of it now. "I can see that aura."

"You're lying!"

"I'm not."

"If you're seeing things, it's down to Ladil's Bloodboil, nothing else."

"It's got nothing to do with the drink!" Something inside Tilda snapped and she lunged across the table to grab Neesha's arm. "Listen to me. I can see the Power, and I think I can feel it too."

"Don't be ridiculous." Neesha tried to pull away.

Tilda tightened her grip. "Will you just shut up and hear me out?" Fear flickered across Neesha's face and Tilda let go, trying not to notice the marks her fingers had left on Neesha's arm. She musn't get angry. She needed to explain, needed Neesha to believe her if they were to stand any chance at all of using this to find the ring.

"Neesha, please listen," she said. "I know it all sounds wrong, but I am telling you the truth. You've just said that the Power can be seen . . . Well, I saw red light around your pendant, the first time I met you. It's glowing right now."

Tears sprang into Neesha's eyes. She shook her head as she tucked her necklace back inside her shirt.

Tilda continued. "I saw the same red light above the washing pans. Saw it around Silviu when I met him. I saw different coloured lights at the Ringstone." She sighed. "Feeling it, well, that's a bit more difficult to explain. When I put my hands into the water in the washing pans, there was a tingle. A bit like after you've had pins and needles. And when Yaduvir and Silviu were fighting…" She paused then, remembering the jolt she'd received. "Energy. I can't explain it better than that."

Neesha looked thoughtful. Had she heard enough to be convinced?

"Show me," she said abruptly, sitting back down and thrusting her half-full cup of water at Tilda. "Stick your fingers in there."

"I don't think—"

"That you can?" Neesha crossed her arms over her chest. "You are so full of rubbish, Tilda."

"I. Am. Not." Tilda gritted her teeth and stuck her index finger into the cup.

"Sure that's enough? You don't want to stick a few more fingers in there?"

Oh, Power, if only she could say what she wanted to . . . Instead, Tilda bit back the reply she really wanted to make, closed her eyes and strained every nerve to detect what she'd felt before. There was nothing. No tingling, no "energy."

Neesha's fingers drummed an impatient tattoo on the table, an unwelcome distraction.

With a real effort, Tilda blocked out the annoying sound and concentrated. Still no tingle. Nothing, in fact, except for her finger feeling cold and wet. Why? Why couldn't she feel anything now?

"There's nothing there," she said quietly, drying her finger on her leggings.

"So you were lying. You can't see or feel anything at all, can you?"

"I can! I . . . Wait a minute . . ." There had been lots more liquid in the pans when she'd detected the tingling—maybe she needed more water? Tilda pulled a jug towards her and plunged her whole hand into it, splashing water all over the table.

"Tilda! What are you—?"

No tingling. And, she realised, suddenly, no red haze either.

A nasty suspicion was growing in Tilda's mind about Neesha's test. "Where does this water come from?" she demanded, pulling her hand out and shaking the water off it.

"Do you mind?" Neesha wiped her face dry. "You've proved you're lying, so don't ask stupid questions." She lifted a leg to swing it over the bench.

Slowly, Tilda stood up and leaned across the table. "I said, where does the drinking water come from? Answer me."

Neesha jumped up and leaned on the table too, pushing her face close to Tilda's. "Don't you dare speak to me like that. When my father hears—"

"That you've been wasting time by tricking me? Yes, I'd like to hear what he'd have to say about that." Tilda was shaking with anger now, didn't care a jot what Silviu might hear from his daughter. "You'd prefer to give me stupid tests instead of listening to me?" She lowered her voice. "I can see and feel the Power. Don't you think that might be rather useful at the moment?"

"You didn't see or feel anything in that water."

"Because it's not the same water that's in the pans, is it?"

Neesha gasped and recoiled, almost as though Tilda had slapped her.

"Thought so." Tilda tried not to look too smug. "I'll ask again. Where does the drinking water come from?"

A range of emotions flickered across Neesha's face, then her shoulders slumped in defeat and she whispered, "A spring nearby."

"And the berry washing water?"

"The Ambak River. About a half hour walk away. The water's piped down to the sheds."

Tilda sank back down onto the bench. "You knew that all along, didn't you?"

Neesha nodded and sat down too. "I needed to make sure. I knew about the Power's aura without ever having seen it. Others might, too. And if they do, they could lie. Say they can see it, when they can't."

"But do you believe *me*?" Tilda held her breath.

Neesha nodded again. "Yes."

Tilda blew out her breath in relief. Thank Power! All she had to do now was work out if she could use this strange ability to find the ring. And why there was Power in the water. And whether the two were linked.

Heavy footsteps interrupted her train of thought. "You two come home tonight?" Abchar rumbled. He looked from Neesha to Tilda and back again, then lowered himself onto the bench beside Neesha. "Why unhappy faces?"

"We haven't found the ring anywhere in the sheds," Neesha told him.

"But . . . we have discovered something that'll help us look for it," Tilda added.

Abchar's eye swivelled between them. "Explain."

So between them, they did.

" . . . but we don't know how the water can be linked to the ring and the Power," Tilda finished. "Unless . . ." Her eyes widened. "You don't think Silviu hid it in the river, do you?"

Neesha pulled a face. "Hardly. It'd be washed downstream with the spring melts. And the river's miles long. It'd take years to search the length of it."

"But there's red light in the water. There has to be a connection." Tilda rested her chin on her hand. "Let's go through what we know again. Silviu said he'd protected the ring, sent it back to its birthplace. We've assumed that's somewhere on the farm because that's where the gateway in the book brought me. But we've looked and it's not here. The only clue we have so far is the red haze I've seen in the river water. Can you think of anything—anything at all—that puts a ring or the Power near the Ambak River?" She looked at Neesha.

"My mother used to tell me a story about the Power." Neesha's voice was so soft, Tilda had to strain to hear it. "How it could be found throughout Issraya and drawn on by those who could detect it. Not everyone used it for good. There were wars between the regions as some individuals tried to harness all of it for their own purposes."

"That's what Yaduvir tried to do," Tilda said, sitting up straighter.

Neesha nodded. "Things got so bad, Issraya was almost destroyed. The regions got so desperate to stop the fighting, they signed a treaty agreeing that the Power should always be shared five ways. Five silviron rings were made and one hidden in each region to absorb the Power from that place. The people who found those rings and brought them back to Ring Isle were the first powermages. And between the hiding and the finding of the rings, the castle on Ring Isle was built. On land not connected to any particular region, where the Power could be drawn on neutral ground and where the rings could be kept safe."

"Where was Ambak's ring found?" Tilda asked, although she thought she could guess.

"Near the Ambak River." Neesha paused and looked thoughtful.

Tilda couldn't help smiling. She'd guessed right. The lost ring *was* connected to the river.

"There's another story about that, though," Neesha said. "That when the first Ambakian mage dug the ring up at the source of the river and washed it, some of the Power ran into the water, seeped into the land, and coloured the berries . . ."

"The source of the river?" Tilda dropped her head into her hands and groaned.

"You not happy with that?"

She looked up at Abchar. "Course I'm not! I might be from the city, but even I know where rivers start. Right up high, in the mountains! I'm going to have to climb a mountain to find the ring."

"You don't have to." Neesha crossed her arms. "Me and Abchar will go. A city girl like you probably wouldn't last more than two minutes in the heights."

Tilda's hands bunched into fists. "Of course I've got to go. How will you find the ring without me? It's me that can feel the Power connected to it, remember?"

"You sure about feeling?" Abchar looked at Tilda.

"Yes." Tilda glared at Neesha.

"In my homeland," Abchar growled, "much done by feelings. Sowing seeds is feelings. Making journey is feelings. Preparing for attack is feelings. Feelings are important."

"But Abchar, she can't do it alone. And if she came with us, she'd slow us down," Neesha argued. "Pa needs that ring back. It's too important to have anything—anyone—delay us. I'm sure we'll be able to find the ring now we know where it is, without Tilda's funny feelings."

Abchar shook his head. "No. Tilda needed. Ring too hard to find without." His eye swivelled round and rested on Tilda. "You say feeling comes when hand is in water?"

She nodded and held her breath. Had she found an ally?

"Then plan is simple. We look after Tilda and walk up river together. Tilda keep putting hand in water until feeling stops. Where feeling stops, there we find ring."

Tilda tried to ignore the angry scowl on Neesha's face. "How far will we have to go, d'you think?"

Abchar grinned. "As far as feeling takes us."

Chapter 18
Into the Mountains

THE NEXT MORNING, Tilda's feeling took her as far as the boundary of the farm. The air was sharp with frost, bright with sunshine, and Bakli came to see them off.

"I can't understand why you'd want to go up into the mountains with winter only just finishin." Bakli shook his head, a frown creasing his brow. "I know you've got Abchar with you, but—"

"We'll be fine." Neesha buttoned the collar on her coat. "I promised to take Tilda higher into the mountains, so we have to go. We'll be back before the berries go down to town."

Tilda shivered. "How long does that give us?"

"A couple of weeks."

"A couple of—?" Power, she was so cold, and her shoulders were already aching from the weight of a rucsac packed with all sorts of outdoorsy equipment and clothing which Neesha had insisted would be needed, she couldn't even think about a couple of *days* in the mountains, let alone a couple of weeks.

"Then I'll save you some space on the wagons." Bakli pulled Neesha into a hug. "You take care of her," he told Abchar when he let her go, and slipped a bottle of something that looked suspiciously like Bloodboil into the giant's pocket. "Silviu won't thank you for losing his daughter in a snowdrift." Then he turned to Tilda. "Enjoy your adventure and make sure to do everything these two tell you. They know these mountains and the conditions, and if you're all to return in one piece . . . Well, safe trip."

For a split second, Tilda considered begging to stay with him on the farm. But only for a second. She *had* to go into the mountains with Neesha and Abchar—they needed her if they were to stand any chance of finding the ring, and she needed them if she was going to survive long enough to help them succeed. With an effort, she pushed thoughts of frostbite and avalanches and wild animals to the back of her mind. The quicker they set off and found the ring, the quicker they could get back and set about rescuing everyone still trapped on Ring Isle.

"Let's go." Neesha grinned, adjusted the straps on her own rucsac and began walking.

Tilda stumbled after Neesha in her borrowed boots, her heavy knee-length coat shortening her stride, the weight on her back forcing her to bend forward. By comparison, Neesha and Abchar looked as though they were out for an afternoon stroll and had already pulled ahead. Tilda gritted her teeth and increased her pace to catch up with them.

The farm buildings were soon left behind, replaced by a broad valley with neat long rows of evergreen bushes planted close together.

"These are all Ambak berry bushes," Neesha called over her shoulder to Tilda, who in spite of her best efforts, was lagging behind. "Can you smell them?"

She certainly could. Walking between the lines, whenever her clothing caught on the branches, a peppery scent rose up from the bruised leaves or broken stems, irritating her nose and making her sneeze.

"You want to try being here when they're all flowering," Neesha said, with a sneeze of her own. "The valley looks beautiful, all pinky-orange, but the smell is a million times worse."

They were almost at the end of the long rows when Tilda heard it; a roaring, growing louder and louder with every step she took, until conversation was almost impossible.

"It's the river," Neesha shouted.

"Where?" Tilda might be able to hear it, but she couldn't see any water.

"Down there!" Neesha yelled, straight into Tilda's ear. She pointed to a dark line in the ground up ahead.

They edged closer. The dark line was actually a deep chasm, and when Tilda leaned over the edge and looked down, there was the Ambak River deep below her, crashing over rocks and boulders and churning itself into white foam.

"Snow's melting," Abchar shouted. "Water high."

"Got to get closer. For Tilda!" Neesha yelled back.

At the thought of getting any closer, Tilda's legs gave way. She fell to her hands and knees, staring down at the nightmare scene. That water would suck her in as soon as she touched it. She'd be swept away, battered against the rocks, drowned... Beads of sweat broke out on her forehead as she crawled backwards, shaking her head. "I can't . . ."

Abchar hauled her to her feet. "I find way down. Stay here." He stepped right up to the very edge of the chasm and leaned over.

"Don't fall," Tilda whispered. "Don't fall."

After a few tense minutes, Abchar indicated that they should all move back. When they were far enough away to speak without shouting themselves hoarse, he told them what he'd found.

"Not easy," he said. "Must climb down to narrow ledge, like a path, above water level."

"Do we have to? Can't we stay up here and still follow the river?" Tilda crossed her fingers and hoped his answer would be yes.

"And how will you use that funny feeling of yours from up here?" Neesha's tone was scornful. "You need to be within reach of the river. Show us the way, Abchar."

He did, and it was terrifying. The rough rocks provided plenty of hand and foot holds as Tilda climbed down, but she couldn't rid herself of the feeling that at any moment, her foot would slip, or the rock she was holding would loosen and fall, plunging her into the icy, roiling water below. Her breath came in sharp gasps, her ears were battered with the noise bouncing off the sides of the chasm, and her palms stung from grazes and cuts, but she kept going, because it was the only way to reach the path that Abchar had spotted.

Except when she reached it, the path was even worse. How was she supposed to walk along a ridge of rock, barely wide enough for one person to stand on? Every one of Tilda's muscles froze.

"Move, Tilda," Neesha screamed at her. "Move!"

A dry sob caught in Tilda's throat as she willed her muscles to respond. Abchar was already some way along the path, moving in a face-to-the-wall, creeping, crab-wise shuffle upstream along the ledge; she took a deep breath, leaned into the chasm's steep side, and mimicked his movements.

She inched along, painfully slowly, for what felt like hours, until suddenly the chasm opened out and the ledge she was standing on broadened. The roar of the river lost some of its volume, thank Power, and it was at long last possible to walk normally.

Tilda almost cried with relief.

The path sloped downwards in front of her, until the water was almost within reach. Almost, but not quite.

Abchar threw himself onto his stomach, and stretching down with his long arm as far as he could, thrust a bottle into the river. By the time Tilda and Neesha reached him, he'd poured the water into a cup.

"Test feeling," he said, handing the cup to Tilda.

The water was bitingly cold, but beneath the burn of that, Tilda's fingers tingled, exactly the same as when she had dipped them into the washing pan. There was Power here, so they still had further to go.

The path twisted and turned, keeping to the chasm's route until eventually it rounded a sharp curve. Tilda stared at the wall of rock ahead of her where the chasm came to an abrupt end. Water poured over the top of it, falling hundreds of feet into a pool so deep, the water was black. Spray rose high into the air and fell like mist on Tilda's coat, coating her in tiny droplets and painting a rainbow in mid-air.

Abchar studied the jumbled rocks on their side of the waterfall, and nodded in satisfaction.

"Easier way up," he announced.

It didn't feel any easier to Tilda. She scrambled and hauled herself up the route Abchar marked out until eventually she stood, bone-weary and exhausted, at the top. A wave of dizziness struck her as she looked back at the water pouring endlessly over the lip and into the chasm below. Thank Power she was finally out of it.

The river above the waterfall was wider, its flow smooth and rapid through a bleak landscape. Gone were the evergreen berry bushes of the lower lands; up here, all was rock and stunted trees and ground that rose in gentle slopes towards steep cliffs and towering snow-topped mountain peaks.

"We eat. Then we walk. Camp there." Abchar pointed.

Tilda squinted. Was that dark green splodge, way ahead, a clump of trees?

She ate quickly, bread and slices of ham washed down with water "from the spring, not the river," Neesha assured her. All too soon, it was time to pull on the heavy rucsac again and start walking towards the place Abchar had chosen for their camp. The muscles in Tilda's legs were aching, her shoulders sore from the straps cutting into them, and her lips dry and chapped from the cold wind blowing across their path. Even so, she tried to keep up with the punishing pace Neesha had set.

Gradually, Tilda fell behind. The gap between her and her companions grew until they were beyond shouting distance, not that she had any spare breath to shout with.

"One . . . step . . . in front . . . of the . . . other," she muttered to herself in time with her footsteps, eyes fixed on the stony ground in front of her feet. "Just . . . keep . . . walking."

The distance to the campsite seemed to be growing instead of shrinking. Tilda's pace slowed to that of a snail. Then nothing at all. She bent almost double under the weight of her rucsac, hands braced against her knees to keep herself from falling onto all fours.

How was she going to carry on? She wasn't used to walking any kind of distance on the flat, let alone in mountains, on hard terrain, and carrying a heavy bag. She should've stayed behind. Tears of frustration blurred her vision. There was no way she could climb any further, let alone find the lost ring—with or without her ability to detect the Power. Issraya would never be saved.

The sound of approaching footsteps forced her to straighten up, groaning at the effort it took. As she pushed her hair out of her eyes, Tilda saw a flash of silver on her wrist. The torc must have slipped down her arm—it was hanging below the edge of her coat. In a panic, she shoved it back under her sleeve, as desperate to keep Neesha from seeing it as she was from showing the mage's daughter how exhausted she was.

But it was Abchar, not Neesha, who'd come back for her. "Eat. You feel better."

Tilda accepted the small packet he offered and unwrapped it. Inside was a lump of something dark red and sticky.

"Eat," Abchar said again.

She bit into the strange substance and chewed. It was dry, yet sweet, and she rolled the unusual taste around her mouth. Within moments of swallowing, fresh strength seemed to seep into her overworked muscles.

"What is this?" She bit off another mouthful.

"Ambakian energy loaf. Made from berries and sugar syrup," Abchar told her, lifting Tilda's pack from her back.

The relief was instant. Tilda rolled her shoulders and rubbed her neck, feeling so much lighter.

Abchar slung her rucsac onto one of his broad shoulders. "Neesha continues." He jerked his head in the direction of the path. "You walk easier now, yes?"

"Yes. Thank you."

"Good. We catch up now."

Abchar matched his pace to Tilda's, shortening his long strides. She was glad of it, because although she no longer had the weight of her bag to slow her down, this section of the path was littered with piles of boulders and rocks, the result of rockfalls from the cliff face to their right. As she picked her way carefully through them, more than once she thought she heard stones slithering and sliding above, and her heart and feet quickened in response. Would a fresh rockfall send both her and Abchar tumbling into the river?

She glanced at her giant companion. He didn't look worried. Perhaps he was too big to be swept away. More likely he'd stop all except the largest of rocks in their tracks. He had to be the biggest, most solid-looking person she'd ever seen, and she'd seen all sorts arriving on the boats in Merjan City. Where did he come from? He reminded her of a pirate she'd seen once, being dragged away to the Academy of Law. That man had been dressed in leather and had an eye patch too. And he'd fought against the Lawmakers every step of the way . . . But as much as Abchar reminded Tilda of the pirate, it was unlikely that a powermage would take a reformed criminal to be his daughter's bodyguard.

Abchar looked down at her, as though he'd felt her stare. "What?"

"Oh! Um . . . I was just wondering . . . You're not from Issraya, are you?"

"No. Abchar from island much far off, Tradora, where all men are born warriors."

She'd never heard of Tradora. It must be many, many miles across the Outer Sea. "Is that why Silviu chose you to look after Neesha, because you're a warrior?"

"I not warrior."

Tilda frowned. How could he not be a warrior, when he looked perfectly capable of breaking bones with his bare hands? "What do you mean?"

"I guard. Different."

Not to Tilda, it wasn't. Surely, whether you were a warrior or a guard, you still had to fight? "Is that how . . . that"—she waved a finger in front of her own eye—"happened? When you were guarding Neesha?"

Abchar's good eye swivelled down, fixing her in its gaze. Then he whipped the patch from his other eye.

Tilda gasped and stumbled over a rock.

The eyeball underneath the patch was perfectly white. No colour, no pupil. Just a shining, blank orb.

"Abchar born this way." Abchar settled the patch back into place. "True Tradoran warrior have two good eyes. My people do not like imperfection, they cover it up and send me away."

"But surely you can still fight with one eye," Tilda said, indignant on his behalf.

"Yes." Abchar looked up suddenly and pointed into the sky. "Look—eagle."

Even squinting, Tilda could only see a dark speck, miles above them. "Are you sure?"

"Abchar have one eye, but is a good one." He laughed and slapped her on the back, sending her staggering half a dozen paces along the path.

"Finally. I was beginning to think you'd got lost."

Tilda looked up and saw Neesha sitting on a rocky outcrop above the path. She didn't even look out of breath. "Perhaps if you'd walked a bit slower—"

"Why should I? I wasn't going any faster than normal. I see you managed to offload your kit."

"Abchar offered to help," Tilda managed to say through gritted teeth. "Unlike someone else I can think of."

Neesha scrambled down from her perch and joined them on the path. "Well, if it means we get to camp sooner rather than later, it's probably a good job."

The sun was dropping behind the mountains when they finally reached the trees they'd been aiming for.

"Camp," Abchar announced. "Soon rest."

It was the best news Tilda had heard all day. She followed Abchar and Neesha, pushing her way through the closely packed pines until they reached a small clearing.

"Tilda, clear floor there for fire. Neesha, set beds out. I cut wood." Abchar disappeared into the trees.

Between them, it took very little time to get a fire going in the makeshift hearth, lay out the padded bedrolls, fry up sausages and bread, and wolf them down. As the circle of sky above her darkened,

Tilda stared into the flames. Maybe that way, she could shut out the inky blackness pressing in on her.

She was used to lit streets, a roof over her head, and cobbles under her feet. Not walls of thick branches, a carpet of pine needles, and a ceiling dotted with the pinpricks of stars and sliced by a thin sliver of moon. It was all too different . . .

Something hooted up in the trees. Tilda jumped.

Neesha sniggered. "An owl won't hurt you. It's the bears and mountain lions you need to worry about."

In spite of the heat from the fire, Tilda went cold. "They won't come here, will they? I mean, animals are frightened of fire. Aren't they?" She tried hard to keep the tremor out of her voice.

"Ha! That's what you think. Last year, the winter was so bad, the bears used to come right down to the farm. They carried off one of the men. All they found was his hat and a few gnawed bones." Neesha's eyes gleamed in the firelight.

Tilda gulped. "And this winter?"

"It was bad," Neesha whispered. "Very bad." Then she burst out laughing "I'm joking! But you should see your face. You're scared stiff."

"I'm not!"

But she was. There were too many strange noises out here. How could she tell if one of them was a bear or a lion, coming to eat her? Her heart thumped hard against her ribs.

"I wouldn't worry too much," Neesha said. "Most animals will avoid you if they hear you coming. But if they don't, climb a tree if you get cornered by a bear. And if it's a lion that finds you, don't run. Make loads of noise and try to make yourself look big."

It sounded easy when Neesha put it that way, but a tight little knot of fear still settled in the bottom of Tilda's stomach.

"Bed," Abchar rumbled.

Tilda wrapped her coat tighter round her body and pulled the hood up. Then she stretched out on her sleeping mat close to the fire, her weight crushing the pine needles underneath until the air was filled with their scent.

Not too long after, Neesha began to snore. Power knew how she managed to fall asleep so easily, because sleep would not come to Tilda; her mind was too full of jumbled thoughts.

What was happening on Ring Isle? Was Yaduvir still safely contained, or had he managed to overcome the other mages? What would he—could he—do to them with his dark magic? What of the ordinary people caught up in the situation? Uncle Vanya and Aunt Tresa, Marja and Stefan and all the other staff? A lump rose in Tilda's throat at the thought of her aunt and uncle. Did they even know what had happened to her? Had Silviu explained? An image of him, staring while the picture in his journal pulled her through the door, jumped into Tilda's head and she shivered. Maybe no-one knew . . . except Silviu.

A log shifted in the fire, sending sparks dancing into the darkness, and Tilda jumped.

"Sleep, Tilda." Abchar had softened his voice so as not to disturb Neesha. "No harm will come."

Chapter 19
A Serious Mistake

THERE WASN'T AN inch of Tilda that didn't hurt the next morning when she rolled off her sleeping mat and tried to stand. She took a few tentative steps and yelped as her calf muscles seized.

"Stiff?" Abchar asked, pulling a loaf of bread from his pack. "Soon wear off. More walk ahead."

She groaned. "I can't. My legs hurt and my heels are blistered!"

"You'd better be able to walk." Neesha finished tying her bootlace and threw something green and damp at Tilda. "Tuck this in your boots. I found it yesterday. It's a moss we use on long journeys. Helps blisters."

Tilda hadn't expected help from Neesha—not after yesterday. "Thank you."

Neesha had started to roll up her sleeping mat. "I'm just trying to find ways of keeping you going. I don't want to be held back any more than I have to be."

Ah. So she wasn't exactly thinking of Tilda, then.

Tilda plonked herself back down on her mat, eased off her boots, and packed them full of moss. She hated to admit it, but her feet felt a hundred times better when she pulled the boots back on.

After breakfast—slices of bacon and cheese between fat slices of toasted dark bread—Neesha pulled a folded parchment from her pack and spread it out on the ground. It was a map.

"We're here," she said, pointing to a thin blue line snaking into white triangles. "We'll carry on up the river, and test the water every hour or so. That way, we won't lose too much time if we have to retrace our steps."

Abchar doused the fire. "We begin."

Tilda swung her packed bag onto her shoulder, almost knocking Neesha over.

"Watch it!" Neesha scowled.

"Sorry." The bag seemed much lighter this morning—but Tilda certainly hadn't imagined its heaviness the previous day. Her aching shoulders were proof of that. She shrugged the other strap on and noticed Abchar staring at her; his eye blinked, slowly and deliberately, before he turned slightly to show her the rucsac he was already carrying. It looked packed to bursting.

He must have taken some of her equipment. "Thank you," Tilda mouthed, hoping that Neesha wouldn't notice.

"So, d'you think you can keep up today, Tilda?" Neesha was pulling on her own bag. "Only for every minute that passes because you're slowing us down, more Power drains from the mages."

"I'll keep up, don't you worry." Tilda tightened the straps and settled her rucsac more comfortably. "And stop reminding me what's happening on Ring Isle," she called as Neesha pushed through the trees back to the path. "I know!" She blew out a frustrated breath. "She doesn't have to rub it in quite so much, when I'm trying to put things right."

"Neesha angry with Power, not you."

Tilda looked at Abchar in surprise. "What do you mean—angry with the Power?"

"Father not with her often. She think, if she proves herself to him, he would be. She jealous of Power for taking him away."

So it wasn't just Tilda who had issues with the Power and certain mages. As she followed Abchar through the trees, she wondered how many other Issrayans did too.

Neesha stuck to her word about making Tilda plunge her hand into the river every hour or so to test for the feeling. They worked their way higher, drawing closer to the snowline, and the water got steadily colder. It was all part of finding the lost ring, Tilda told herself each time she gritted her teeth against the burning cold, waiting for the all-important tingle. Occasionally, she spotted the red haze shimmering above the water's surface, which meant she barely had to touch the liquid before announcing that yes, they were still on the right track, but had further to go.

It was getting harder and harder to make good progress. Tilda took three steps forward and slid two back on slopes of loose scree. She jumped over frequent rivulets caused by snowmelt running into the river. She grazed her hands scrambling over huge boulders, and her ankles ached from tripping over smaller rocks.

Several mountain goats watched her painful progress, balancing perfectly on almost sheer rock faces. Tilda cursed them under her breath, especially when they leapt easily from rock to rock, ridiculing with bleating cries her own rather pathetic attempts to do the same. They weren't the only wildlife she saw; once, there was the lumpy shape of a bear in the distance, and Tilda offered hasty thanks to the Power that the bear hadn't seen or smelt them and changed direction. And how she wished that she, too, had wings, as she watched eagles circling effortlessly over her head.

By late morning, a mixture of fatigue, hunger, and cold was beginning to take its toll. The air up here felt thin; Tilda's breaths were coming faster and harder as she toiled behind Neesha. They were well above the snowline now, and forced to wade through thick drifts of snow. Whenever Neesha decided it was time to check the river, Abchar held on tightly to the back of Tilda's coat while she leaned out over its frozen edges to reach the running water.

"Fall in, you freeze," he growled at her.

"L-l-l-like I'm n-n-not already?" Tilda's teeth were chattering so much, it was hard to speak. "Pull me b-b-b-ack. We n-n-n-eed to c-c-ca-carry on."

"Are you sure? You can still feel it?" Neesha asked, slapping her arms against her body to keep the blood circulating.

"Yes. I almost w-w-wish I couldn't, then we'd kn-n-now we'd gone too f-f-far and could t-t-t-turn back." Tilda shoved her glove back on, taking the opportunity to push the torc back up inside her sleeve. It kept slipping down, and the last thing she wanted was to lose it up here in the snow. She really ought to put it into her bag for safekeeping, but the metal always felt warm against her skin, no matter how cold the rest of her was. If only she could have slipped it into her glove, to warm up her cold-numbed fingers.

"Those clouds are full of snow." Neesha sighed. "We'd best carry on as long as we can, before we set up camp."

Tilda looked round at the rocks and snow. There was no shelter here, so where was Neesha proposing they camped? "Where are we g-going to do that?"

Neesha crossed her arms. "Anywhere we can find a large enough pocket of snow. Abchar will make an ice cave."

"Sleep in the ice? We'll freeze to death!" Panic squeezed Tilda's throat, making her voice squeak.

"Ice cave soon warm up with heat from bodies," Abchar rumbled. "Cosy."

Tilda's mind felt as numb as her fingers and toes as they carried on walking, and she tried not to think about sleeping in a cave made of ice.

The first icy flake to land on her cheek set her shivering uncontrollably.

Neesha swore. "Keep moving," she snapped. "It's not snowing badly."

As if to prove her wrong, the snow began to fall steadily, thick and feather-like, enveloping Tilda in a silent blanket of white. She tucked her head deep inside her hood and trudged on, one foot in front of the other, determined not to stop until Neesha or Abchar said they should. She felt like a walking snowman by the time they reached a snowmelt tributary far too wide for even Abchar to jump across.

As the snow swirled around them, Abchar manhandled several large rocks into the running water, creating a line of stepping stones which they all crossed carefully. On the far side of the water, snow lay waist-deep and unbroken. Abchar forced his mighty frame through it, making a narrow path that still roughly followed the main course of the river.

Tilda followed Abchar, the cold cutting through to her bones. Snow was everywhere; it whirled around her head, squeaked under her feet, and coated her eyelashes until she could barely see. She had lost track of time, had no idea how long they had walked in the blizzard—hours, probably—when she realised with a shock that the snow was easing.

Abchar called a halt. He pointed to a large outcrop of rock a way off to their right and away from the river, under which a massive snowdrift had formed. "Make cave there, rest."

Tilda would have cried with relief, but she did not want her tears to freeze on her cheeks. Instead she followed the new path that Abchar made, which took them away from the river.

As soon as they reached the drift under the rock, Abchar set about using his gloved hands as spades, digging into the snow. He scooped it out, creating a deep hole, and directed Neesha and Tilda to pound and shape the loose stuff into a windbreak across the entrance. Tilda was sweating by the time they all crawled into the finished cave.

Abchar settled himself against the back wall and opened his rucsac. He drew out a small stove and a tightly corked bottle of liquid fuel.

"For emergency," he said, his eye twinkling in the fading daylight. "Sleeping in ice—emergency."

The temperature in the cave rose, thanks to the stove and the heat of three bodies. It was still cold, but warmer than outside; Tilda could at least take off her coat. A hasty dinner of sliced sausage and fried bread, followed by a drop of Bloodboil diluted in melted snow, warmed her insides, too.

Neesha raised her cup in a toast. "Here's to Tilda's fingers, which have kept us on the right track. May tomorrow be the day we get even closer to the ring and to saving the powermages and . . ."

Tilda's stomach gave a painful lurch. Oh, Power. She had completely forgotten to test the river while they fought through the blizzard. When *had* she last dipped her fingers in the water?

Neesha fell silent and slowly lowered her cup. "Why are you looking like that, Tilda?" Her voice was heavy with suspicion.

Tilda gulped. "I—well, I . . . I'm trying to remember when I last checked the river." If only she could hide from the three eyes staring at her. It wasn't her fault, it had been snowing, and–

Neesha's tone lowered the temperature in the cave by several degrees. "Exactly *when* did you last test it?"

"Um . . ." Tilda racked her brain. "I think . . . yes . . . When Abchar held me over the water. It started snowing soon after." Her cheeks were burning, which had nothing at all to do with the heat from Abchar's little stove.

"We've covered miles since then," Neesha said, her voice hollow. "Are you telling me that we walked all that way and you didn't check once?"

Tilda tried to defend herself. "It was snowing, and no-one reminded me and—"

"Get out there and test the water. Now."

"What? I'm not going out there now—it's almost dark."

"Tough. We need to know." Neesha was trembling with anger.

Tilda couldn't blame her. She was ashamed of herself. What if they had to backtrack most of that way? She'd been so careful to check the water every hour or so before that point, so they wouldn't have to retrace their steps too far if she got to a place where she couldn't detect the Power's tingle. "Can't we wait until morning? I mean, we can't walk anywhere tonight, can we?" Tilda looked to Abchar for support, but found none in the giant's sombre expression.

Tears filled her eyes. Without a word, she pulled on her coat and crawled out of the cave, gasping as the chill air hit her cheeks. She hauled herself to her feet and took a moment to get her bearings. The light was fading, but there was still enough reflecting off the snow to see the tracks she'd made such a short time ago.

As Tilda followed them back down to the river, she argued with herself. She should've checked. Even in all that snow, she should've checked. But they'd all been so focussed on keeping going through the storm—and no-one else had thought about it or reminded her, had they? So it wasn't fair to blame it all on her, was it? Fancy forcing her to check now. A part of her hoped she'd still be able to feel the familiar tingle, so she could go straight back and tell Neesha how daft she'd been, getting all worked up for no reason, because they still had further to go . . .

Turning her anger towards Neesha was easier than feeling ashamed. Tilda got as close as she dared to where she thought the edge of the river was hidden under fresh snow. She cleared a small area until she found a rock, big enough to kneel on and reach the water safely. Then she knelt, took a deep breath, ripped off her glove and stuck her hand into the river.

She stayed like that until her fingers were blue and numb, and the last glimmer of daylight had disappeared from the sky.

There was no tingle here. The water was freezing, but it wasn't touched with Power. They had come too far.

Tilda pushed her near-frozen fingers back into her glove and dragged her shivering body back to the cave, dreading what Neesha and Abchar would say. She'd barely stuck her head inside when Neesha pounced.

"Well?"

Tilda collapsed next to the stove, pulled off her glove, and held out her pale, cold fingers to the meagre flames.

"We've come too far," she whispered.

"You idiot, Tilda! We could've perhaps found the ring by now."

"I'm sorry." Tilda chewed her lip and shoved her hand into her armpit as hot aches started to burn her fingertips. "I messed up. But now we know we're close, have a definite stretch of the river we can search."

Neesha didn't answer; simply lay down and turned her back on Tilda.

"We're close," Tilda repeated, hoping to Power she was right.

Chapter 20
Oxala

TILDA EMERGED FROM the ice cave the next morning to a sparkling white world. The sun was shining, the air was clear, but she felt as though storm clouds were still sitting over her head. Neesha hadn't said a word to her since they'd woken, and even Abchar's conversation—usually short and to the point—was non-existent.

She'd check the river a million times today, if it meant they started speaking to her again.

"For Power's sake," Neesha exploded, as Tilda stopped for the twentieth time, having barely taken a hundred paces back down the river. "If you're going to stop this often, we'll never get anywhere today. Spread it out a bit, will you?"

"Sorry," Tilda mumbled, yanking her hand out of the water. "I just don't want to miss the point where things change. I—"

"Look, we're going to be crossing the stones soon. Can you at least hold back until we get to that point? Until then, just . . . keep walking!" Neesha spun away and strode on.

"Yes . . . I can do that."

But the temptation to check a couple of times more, especially when Neesha wasn't looking, was too strong. There was no tingling, no colour, and Tilda felt even worse as she realised how far she'd brought them all beyond where they needed to be.

When they reached the tributary where Abchar had made the crossing, the water was running higher and faster over and around the stones. Yesterday's snow must be melting, adding to the volume.

Tilda checked the river: still nothing.

"And still we have to go back over ground already covered," Neesha snapped, leaping onto the first stepping stone.

Tilda's whole body tensed. "Careful!"

"What?" Neesha spun towards her on a rock slick with water. "Scared I might fall? No chance." She jumped from stone to stone—feet slip-sliding but never enough to completely lose balance—until she reached the far side of the stream, where she stood, safe, dry, and laughing at Tilda.

Abchar crossed just as easily, hardly even needing to break his stride.

When both of them started to walk away, showing no sign of waiting for her, Tilda eyed the wet stones with distrust. There was no other way over, she had to do this. And if she slipped and fell, well, the water wasn't really that deep. The worst she might end up with was a wet boot. Or possibly two. It'd be uncomfortable, certainly, but at least she'd be on the other side . . .

She took a deep breath, and jumped onto the first stone. She landed well, her feet remaining dry. Her breath blew out in a whoosh of relief. This was easy. She grinned and leapt forward onto the second stone, again onto the third.

Her foot slid out from under her.

She went down on one knee, cracking it against the wet stone. Off balance, she tipped sideways and threw out a hand to stop herself from falling into the stream; she ended up wrist deep in the freezing water and looked down in shock.

A snake writhed around her submerged wrist.

A snake?

Tilda yanked her hand out of the water so fast, she almost fell into the stream backwards. She tugged at the creature, panting, trying to pull it off and—

Suddenly, it dawned on her what she was fighting to rid herself of. She began to laugh. Except it wasn't really a laugh, more a cross between a frightened sob and hysterics.

"It's the torc, that's all. The torc," she gasped. Her fall must've dislodged it, sent it sliding below her coat cuff. It was the rippling water that had made it look as though it was moving. How ridiculous to think it was alive. Of course it wasn't, however much the tiny black eyes glittered at her when she dried it and pushed it back up her arm. "I'm such an idiot."

Still perched precariously on the rock in the middle of the stream, Tilda turned her attention to her injuries; a purple bruise already coming up and visible through the tear in her leggings, and a cut on her hand—right across the palm—still running with blood. She'd have to wash that off before she put her glove back on.

She gritted her teeth and lowered her hand into the water again. At first, she put the tingling down to the cut, and the pink tinge in the water to the blood. But as the tingling got stronger, she saw . . . well, she thought she saw . . . yes, she could definitely see . . .

Red light, above the water. The more she looked, the more she could see it. On the far side of the stream, it was thick like treacle, darker than she'd ever seen it before.

It was here. The ring was here, somewhere near this stream.

Tilda scrambled to her feet, and opened her mouth to call Neesha and Abchar, let them know what she'd found. But then she closed it again as she became aware of a gentle pulling sensation, pulling away from the river they'd all been so intent on following.

What was this feeling? Tilda could see and feel Power in the water, but this was something new. Was it Power-related too? Seeping from the ring, telling her which way to go? If so, the ring must be close.

What if she could find it on her own? For one blissful moment, Tilda allowed herself to imagine the look on Neesha's face if she did.

The pulling sensation grew stronger; it felt as though someone had hooked a cord onto her belt and was gently drawing her up the course of the stream.

She had to decide. Call the others back and involve them in the next step of the search? Or carry on alone, trusting that she'd guessed right about the pull and its source?

She'd do it on her own.

Carefully, Tilda crossed the rest of the stream. On the far side, she shot a last glance towards Neesha and Abchar, then struck out on a new path beside the snowmelt stream. She didn't get far before it narrowed, thinned to a trickle, and disappeared at a point between some larger rocks peeping out from the snow. The ruby-tinged water sprang up between them, as though by magic. Was this the place? The source of the Ambak River, the place where Neesha's legend said the ring had originally been found?

Tilda flung her rucsac down and dropped to all fours, wincing as her already bruised knee hit the ground. She tugged at the rocks, working them loose and throwing them aside in her haste to find the ring.

She didn't find anything. Yet the water still carried the colour, indicating that the ring must be somewhere close. She sat back on her heels, frustrated, and looked around. Where else could it be, if it wasn't here? Actually, now she'd stopped moving the rocks, she could still feel that gentle tug, but to where, exactly?

Then she saw what she'd been searching for; a little way further up the slope, the sun had melted the snow and left a few rocks dry. Between those rocks were glimmers of red light. The reason was so obvious—how could Tilda have missed it?

"The water's still running underneath the snow," she gasped.

Starting from this new point, she tracked the red light back further. Sometimes she lost it and was forced to clear an area of snow until she picked up the trail again. It was slow work, but the continued presence of the light over the water and the constant pull at her navel kept her moving uphill.

Until the water *and* the light disappeared completely underneath an enormous boulder.

Tilda groaned. The boulder was taller than Abchar and as wide as her bedroom on Ring Isle. If the ring was under this, she'd never be able to get to it, not even with Abchar and Neesha to help. They—

High above her head, something growled.

The hairs on the back of Tilda's neck rose. Hardly daring to breathe, she looked up at the top of the boulder.

An animal's head was silhouetted there, against the sky.

Tilda's ribcage vibrated, a combination of her pounding heart and the animal's continuous low growl. Was it a lion? Oh, Power. She tried to swallow the bitter fear rising up from her stomach, but her throat was too tight and dry.

For long, stretched seconds, neither she or the lion moved.

Then Tilda dared one teeny-tiny step away from the boulder, fighting against every instinct screaming at her to run.

The growling stopped. In a single graceful leap, the huge grey cat landed at the base of the boulder, a short distance from where Tilda stood. An image of Silviu, dressed in his winter coat, flashed across her mind; this wasn't a lion.

The oxala stared at Tilda. Its ears flattened against its skull, purple eyes darkening as the pupils dilated. Its tail switched back and forth like a whip, and it dropped to its belly, haunches quivering.

Then it pounced.

Tilda leapt backwards. A stone turned under her heel, sending a stab of white hot pain through her ankle. She crashed to the ground, her head slamming against a rock. Sparkling lights exploded in her vision, filling the world with fireworks as a deafening roar blew warm, moist air against her cheek.

The roaring stopped. Was that shouting Tilda could hear instead? Through the mass of stars dancing past her eyes, she could see the oxala crouching beside her. It didn't seem interested in her at the moment; it was looking away, back towards the river and the noise. Biting back a groan, Tilda turned her head in the same direction.

Was that Abchar, bounding up the slope, whirling his coat round and round above his head, shouting and cursing in a language she didn't understand? Yes, it was. When he skidded to a halt, Tilda slowly turned her aching head back towards the oxala; it was watching her again, and far too close for comfort when it blinked.

There were flecks of grey in those purple eyes, Tilda realised.

Abchar let out a deafening roar.

The oxala flinched, its head snapping back towards the giant, lips drawn back in a silent snarl.

Those incisors are as long as my little fingers, Tilda thought, as she heard Abchar growling deep in his throat as he crunched on the snow behind her.

For a long time, the oxala stared at him. Then it rose fluidly to its feet and padded away without a backward glance.

Tilda let out the breath she hadn't realised she'd been holding and allowed her head to fall back. She stared at the blue sky above her.

"Lucky escape," Abchar rumbled, lifting her up and setting her on her feet.

"You idiot!" Neesha yelled, white-faced and quivering. "What were you thinking, going off on your own? If Abchar hadn't turned back, seen your tracks . . . When the oxala leapt and you fell, I thought—"

"Quiet," Abchar snapped.

Tilda wasn't listening. Her head was throbbing, her ears buzzing. She touched the back of her skull gingerly. "Ow!"

"You bleed? Let me see."

Abchar gently probed the sorest place on Tilda's scalp, making her wince, but there was no sign of blood. "Soon heal, though headache might take while to go."

There was more than pain hammering away inside Tilda's head. There was something she had to say, something important. She shook her head, trying to clear it, and regretted the movement immediately.

"The river," she managed to say.

"Yes, it's way back there." Neesha flung an arm out. "Where you should be, looking for the ring."

"No . . . it's here . . . under the snow . . . saw it . . ."

"Saw the ring?" Neesha frowned and looked at Abchar. "Is she delirious?"

"It ends . . . starts . . . here." She'd show them, that'd be easier. Tilda took one step towards the boulder and her twisted ankle collapsed under her, sending sharp needles shooting up her leg. Abchar caught her before she hit the ground and she clung to his arm, breathless with pain.

"Oh, that is all we need. We're this close"—Neesha pinched her thumb and forefinger together until they almost touched—"this close to finding the ring, and you can't walk?"

"Fetch bags," Abchar said.

Neesha put her hands on her hips. "Excuse me?"

"Fetch bags," he repeated. "We stop here. Tilda need to rest."

Neesha shot Tilda a venomous glance and stomped off.

Tilda was in so much pain, she barely noticed.

Chapter 21
Discovery

IN SPITE OF the pain from her ankle and head, that night, Tilda slept and dreamed.

. . . She was standing beside the enormous boulder, staring at the thread of water and red light disappearing under it.

"Hello, Teeel-da."

. . . turning to face . . .

. . . Yaduvir . . .

"Give me the ring, Teeel-da."

. . . holding her hands open . . . "I haven't got it."

. . . Yaduvir snarling . . . muttering ancient, nasty words . . .

. . . fear . . . acid . . . bitter . . . rising in her throat . . .

. . . watching the mage sink onto all fours, body melting and morphing until . . .

. . . he is an oxala . . . with eyes as black as night . . .

. . . which leaps at her—

Tilda jolted awake, gasping. "No!"

"You dream," Abchar muttered. "Go back to sleep." He rolled over, and was soon snoring again.

There'd be no more sleep for Tilda, not now. Abchar was supposed to have been keeping watch, in case the oxala came back. If he was sleeping, she'd rather stay awake, especially after the dream she'd just had. Yaduvir changing into an oxala . . . She shuddered, hoping that his dark magic wasn't enough to let him do that for real.

Why had she dreamt of him? It would've been more useful to dream about how she was going to get the ring out from under this stupid rock.

As the sky grew lighter, Tilda's mind turned to the thread of red light disappearing under the boulder—both in the dream and in reality—and the pulling sensation which had drawn her to it. Was the source of the Ambak River actually underneath this giant slab of grey granite? Hang on, underneath—

"Morning." Neesha yawned, and rolled over to face Tilda. "How's your ankle?"

"Um, I don't know." She didn't want to think about her ankle, she wanted to think about water, about its ability to run under snow and ice . . . and perhaps under rocks, too . . .

"Perhaps you ought to take a look at it?"

Tilda pulled aside the bandage Abchar had improvised, grimacing as she revealed the purple and blue bruising underneath.

"That looks awful." Neesha frowned.

"It does." Tilda circled her foot slowly. Didn't feel too bad, though.

"Can you walk on it?"

She crawled off her sleeping mat and used the boulder to pull herself to her feet. Then she tried a few steps; it was uncomfortable, but not impossible, to walk. She glanced down. The line of red light—no thicker than a string, yet vividly coloured—was easy to spot. Shivers of excitement rippled along her skin.

"I'm going to go for a walk round this rock," she said, trying to keep the eagerness out of her voice as Abchar snorted and opened a bleary eye. "Try my ankle out properly."

Neesha nodded. "I'll get breakfast ready."

Tilda's mind worked quickly as she limped around the boulder, gritting her teeth every time her damaged ankle took her weight. If water was able to run under snow and ice and small rock piles, maybe it could run under large rocks, too. Just because it looked as though the aura-tinted water came from underneath the boulder didn't mean it actually *started* at that point. There could be a spring, further up the mountain, behind this huge lump of stone, and the water had taken a subterranean route rather than run round. "Going for a walk" would let her check this theory. If she was right, there'd be another line of light on the rock's far side somewhere, and she'd tell the others. If she was wrong, well, she wouldn't say anything and they'd just have to start digging—

Without warning, the ground disappeared in front of Tilda. She windmilled her arms as she teetered on the edge of a small natural basin, about as deep as she was tall. At the bottom of the basin was a bubbling pool of clear water with a dark red haze shimmering above it.

Tilda sat down heavily, not trusting her legs to hold her up. "Thank Power," she whispered.

With absolute, utmost certainty, she knew that *this* was the place where the mighty Ambak River began. This little spring in its own pool was its true source—and she only had to look at the aura to know that the missing ring had to be here, too.

But where exactly? There were so many crevices between the rocks, it would take ages to search every one for the ring, even with Neesha and Abchar's help.

Did they need to do that though? Could she use the tell-tale red light to focus her search instead? Although disappointingly, there wasn't any hint of it around the sides of the basin—it was only over the water. No, wait! There . . . A bush of some sort, growing right at the water's edge, almost opposite where she was sitting. It looked like one of the bushes she'd seen back at the farm—there were even a few scarlet berries hanging from its branches. How had an Ambak berry bush grown all the way up here?

The answer to that question wasn't important though; Tilda's mouth fell open as she realised there was red light—snaking out of the ground at the base of the bush, wrapping tendrils of itself around the knotted and twisted trunk.

"Oh, Power," she breathed.

Not only had she found the source of the Ambak River. She'd found the exact place where the aura was running into the water.

Which could only mean one thing; the ring was here.

Ignoring the twinges from her ankle, Tilda slid into the basin and scrambled around it until she could lower herself down beside the bush. She took a deep breath, and reached towards the red light.

As soon as her fingers made contact, a tendril wrapped around her hand. Her fingers tingled and once again she had the strangest sensation of being wrapped in warm blankets. Her entire body fizzed with energy and the ache in her ankle faded. Against her arm, the torc grew warmer and warmer until it was almost unbearably hot.

Pure Power—but should she be touching it? Tilda pulled her hand away slowly, reluctant to break contact. The light stretched and thinned until it broke, leaving her feeling oddly bereft and with an aching ankle once more. She sat and watched the light pouring into the pool for a moment or two, thinking.

The ring must be buried. In the ground, under the bush. Like in the legend.

"But it's going to be me who digs it up, this time." Tilda snatched up a sharp stone and, working methodically, scraped at the soil around the bush, freeing its roots and pushing the loose earth away quickly so she wouldn't miss any glimmer of silviron.

"I brought you breakfast."

Tilda stopped digging and looked up.

Neesha was standing on the edge of the basin, holding out half a sausage and a slice of bread. "You didn't come back, so I thought I'd better come and find you. What are you doing?"

"Nothing. Thanks." Tilda washed the mud from her hands, accepted the food and started eating.

Neesha tried again. "It's not nothing. It looks like you're digging up that Ambak berry bush."

Tilda chewed and swallowed. This should have been *her* moment, where she could begin to put right the trouble she'd caused. Where she was the one to recover the ring. Why couldn't Neesha have waited another few minutes before coming to find her? She could hardly dig the ring up with her standing there. She'd have to explain.

"I'm looking for the ring."

"And you think *this* is the right place?" Neesha sounded doubtful. "It's not even on the river."

"I know, but the aura led me here. I can see red light coming up from under the bush." Her voice dropped to a whisper. "I touched it."

Neesha didn't respond, simply pulled her locket out of her shirt and ran it up and down its chain in a familiar gesture.

Tilda finished her breakfast, brushed the crumbs off her leggings, and went back to digging.

"Do you want some help?" Neesha asked.

No, she didn't *want* it. But if it meant the digging time was halved, well, she was willing to accept it. She handed Neesha a stone and side by side, they dug. The torc had slipped down Tilda's wrist again, the snake's head peeping out from her cuff, but this time she left it where it was. It seemed right to have Silviu with her—in spirit at least—when they finally recovered the ring. As she glanced down at the torc, she caught the glint of light on metal in the corner of her eye.

Every muscle in her body seized.

The ring was half-buried in the soil at the bottom of the hole she'd dug, caught between the tangled roots of the bush. Thick red light oozed from it.

Tilda's stone spade fell into the pool with a splash.

"Tilda? What is it?"

Using her fingers, Tilda set about teasing the ring from its earthy prison, her skin prickling at the contact. "I've found it," she whispered, hardly daring to believe it was true.

"Are you sure? Show me."

The ring came free, and she tried to brush away the mud still clinging to it. With a jolt, she realised that the red light hanging over the pool had changed; the surface still bubbled with the water feeding it, but the redness was fading, as though it was being washed away. Was that because the ring had been found? It didn't need to keep feeding Power into the water as a clue to its hiding place?

With a growing sense of wonder, Tilda lowered the ring into the pool, watching as the mud melted away into the water. When every trace of earth had disappeared, she lifted it, dripping, from the pool.

The ring pulsed gently with red light, and Tilda was sure her heart was pulsing in time with it.

"Look," she said, glancing up.

Neesha was gripping her pendant tightly and staring, horrified, at something she could see over Tilda's shoulder.

"Hello, Teeel-da."

With the voice came a lump of something leaden, dropped from a great height and landing in Tilda's stomach. Her hand closed tight around the ring as she turned, slowly.

She was back in her dream. How else could she explain Yaduvir being here, leaning casually against the huge boulder? Except she couldn't be dreaming—she was wide awake. Her skin prickled, this time with fear. If this was real, how had he found her? Before she could ask, Yaduvir's outline shimmered; for the time it took to blink twice, he became insubstantial, misty. Then he solidified again, causing a dark shadow to fall over the pool.

"You have found the ring," he said.

"Abchar!" Tilda screamed. Except the sound was muffled, barely more than a whisper. She tried to scramble out of the basin, away from the pool and the powermage, but her limbs were heavy, wouldn't obey her. At the edge of her vision was Neesha, mouth open in a silent scream, hand still gripping her pendant, motionless.

"I ought to point out that I have magic at my disposal that you cannot imagine, Teeel-da." Yaduvir pushed himself away from the rock and walked closer. His footsteps seemed to barely touch the ground; they did not move a single stone. "The giant won't hear you and the girl can't move . . . so it's just the two of us. Isn't that nice?" He tilted his head to one side. "I've been watching you, Teeel-da, ever since your sudden disappearance from Ring Isle."

Tilda's mind was racing. How could he be here? Did this mean he'd overcome the other mages? Forced Silviu to make another doorway? Or had he found another way, using dark magic? Then she realised what Yaduvir had said.

"Watching me?"

"All the time." Yaduvir leaned closer, his black eyes dancing with amusement. "You did well to keep up with your companions, out here in the wild. I'd have been tempted to stay at the berry farm, myself. Much more comfortable than sleeping in the open, or braving a blizzard." He sat down on a large rock.

Except that he didn't actually sit; Tilda could see several inches of space between his backside and the stone. How could he be floating?

"I thought you'd had it when the oxala pounced, I really did," Yaduvir continued, shaking his head. "Power bless the giant for scaring it off, eh?"

Tilda opened and closed her mouth, but nothing came out of it. She tried again. All she could think of to say was, "How?"

Yaduvir tapped the side of his nose and he grinned. "You can't expect me to reveal everything at once, Teeel-da. I must be allowed some secrets. My mentor has made it possible for me to leave Ring Isle and approach you in this...spirit form. You cannot imagine the feeling, Teeel-da!" Suddenly his outline shivered, his smile fading as the edges of his robes disintegrated and trailed raggedly around him. He frowned and stood up, one hand outstretched towards Tilda. "Enough. I do not have much time left. Give me that ring."

Tilda recoiled. "Never."

Yaduvir closed his eyes and sighed. "I was hoping I wouldn't have to do this . . ." His eyes shot open, and he fixed their blackness on Tilda. "Exstreyth kadrak, livazda mortran . . ."

Tilda's arm moved. She tried to resist, her fist and the ring in it shaking as she fought the command in the words. She might have succeeded too, but as her hand reached shoulder height, a silver body slithered out of her sleeve.

She screamed as the impossible creature coiled around her wrist, its flesh hot against her skin. The tiny head rose, stared at her with those glittering stone eyes and blinked, once. Then the coils tightened, and Tilda screamed again as increasing pressure ground her bones together and forced her fingers to peel open like a flower.

Yaduvir's face twisted into a victorious grin as Tilda's last finger uncurled, revealing the ring. He glided closer, until he was almost within touching distance. "Estrayk alambra brethmeryk," he growled and reached out to take the ring.

Tilda could do nothing to stop him. She was helpless, watching as Yaduvir's hand became more distinct, more solid than the rest of him, the creases in his skin and the soft sheen of his nails as visible to her now as they had been when he had stood in front of her in the Welcome Room.

Without warning, a dark feathered shape dived at Tilda, tearing the silver snake from her wrist.

Yaduvir threw up his arms and twisted away with a shout.

Tilda felt his magic release her and dived to the ground as the huge black bird swooped for a second time, so close, she could see its brilliant yellow eyes and wickedly curved talons—talons which dropped the silver snake by her feet.

She scrambled away from it, gasping, fearing it would attack again. But all that remained of Silvu's torc was a bent and broken metallic corpse.

The bird called, a harsh "keee-aauuw" as it rose swiftly into the air. Then it plummeted again—this time, towards Yaduvir.

Yaduvir yelled and tried to swat the bird away. A storm of black feathers fluttered around him and Tilda blinked. Were they really flashing with red sparks?

The attack was having an effect on Yaduvir. His whole body began to fade, becoming hazy and faint. It was like watching heavy smoke from a bonfire being thinned by the wind.

"If I can't have the ring, I shall destroy—" With a final shriek, he vanished.

"Wha-what just happened? Who was that?" Neesha gasped. She looked as though she'd just woken from a nightmare.

"Yaduvir." Tilda scrambled to her feet, wincing as she put weight onto her injured ankle. A strong, persistent tingling ran up her arm from her clenched fist. Slowly, she opened her hand.

The metallic particles in the silviron glinted as the ring was exposed to the light.

Neesha gasped. "Oh, thank Power! I thought he'd taken it." Her brow crinkled. "How did he know you'd found it?"

Tilda nudged the broken snake with her toe. "I think he did something to this. He gave it to Silviu, it was the only one with stone eyes . . ." Her own eyes widened as she realised the truth. "He was watching me—us—all the while, through the snake. He saw me find the ring!"

"That belonged to Pa? Then why did you—?" Neesha stopped and shook her head. "I don't want to know why you had it. That's not important. What is important is that it's useless now, and Yaduvir can't spy on us." She shivered.

"And it's useless thanks to the bird—oh!"

As if it had been called, the huge black bird swooped low over Tilda's head. It landed on the berry bush, where it perched, yellow eyes unblinking.

"Don't make any sudden moves," Neesha whispered. "It's a Black Mountain Eagle, can tear a goat apart."

As she was talking, the eagle stretched its wings wide. There was something not quite right about the left one; it looked ragged, as though it were missing a few—

Tilda gasped. "Silviu's eagle!"

"What?"

"The wing, see it?" Tilda looked at Neesha. "It's exactly the same as on his initiation robe."

Neesha clutched her pendant again, eyes widening in disbelief. "How could he make it real?"

Together, Tilda and Neesha turned to look at the bird. As though it had been waiting for their attention, it lifted one of its feet.

"Look! There's something tied to its leg," Neesha hissed. There was; a small roll of . . . "Parchment?"

Could this really be Silviu's eagle? Tilda didn't understand, but the bird was there, right in front of her, as real as Neesha standing by her side. Had it been created it using the Power to help whoever found the ring? If so, and that tiny roll of parchment held a message, then Tilda had to read it. She eyed the eagle's sharp beak, slipped the ring into her pocket, and inched closer to the eagle.

"Be careful!"

Tilda kept her eyes on the giant bird and moved slowly, carefully, towards it. The eagle watched her, and apart from blinking, it did not move. With trembling fingers, Tilda untied the thread which held the parchment in place and teased the roll free.

As though her action had released it, the eagle took off from the bush so abruptly, Tilda sat down, hard. She watched it rise into the air with a loud "keee-aauuw" and, with a flash of red, disappeared.

"Are you alright?"

"I'm fine." Tilda pushed herself to her feet. "A few more bruises, that's all." She rubbed her backside and checked her pocket, to make sure the ring hadn't fallen out. "Let's have a look at this." She unrolled the parchment, which looked as though it had been torn from the corner of a page. There were only two lines written on it, in a handwriting she recognised.

Neesha peered over Tilda's shoulder. "What does it say?"

Not what Tilda thought it would; this was no offer of help for the ring-finder. It was a message—for Neesha.

"'Neesha, the words will bring you to me,'" Tilda said, frowning. "Then there's more. In a language I don't know, with your name in the middle of it." She looked up. "I don't understand."

Neesha had forgotten to put her pendant away; it lay outside of her jacket, still glowing. Tilda stared at it. Silviu had put Power into it, to keep Neesha safe—wasn't that what Neesha had said? And she had been holding it when Yaduvir appeared. If it was possible to make a picture of a door open and transport a person hundreds of miles using the Power, was it also possible to enchant objects to do the same?

Tilda pointed. "Your necklace."

"What about it?"

"I think Silviu definitely put Power in it. Enough so that if you were ever in danger, the eagle would appear to give you this message." She held up the parchment. "This is a way to go straight to your father. It's another doorway, like the one in the journal."

Neesha snatched the parchment from Tilda's hand. "We have to tell Abchar. Come on!"

Tilda limped as fast as she could round the boulder, trying to keep up.

"Abchar, Tilda's found the ring!" Neesha shouted, waving the slip of parchment in the air. "But Yaduvir tried to take it, then Pa's eagle arrived and stopped him. There's a message and—"

"Stop!" Abchar dropped the bag he was in the middle of repacking and held up a hand. "Explain. Slowly."

Between the two of them, they did. Abchar's eye grew wider the more they told him, and he growled so deep in his throat when they told him what Yaduvir had tried to do, Tilda thought for one horrible moment that the oxala had returned.

"So now we've got the ring, I can take it to Pa, straightaway," Neesha finished, her face flushed with excitement.

"Hang on a minute. Why you?" Tilda pressed her hand against the ring in her pocket. "I was the one who spoiled Silviu's plans in coming through the journal instead of him, and it was me who found the ring. It's *my* responsibility to take it back to Ring Isle."

"But the enchantment names me, not you, so it's me who can go back, not you. With the ring." Neesha held out her hand.

Oh, no. That's not how it was going to work. Tilda's blood boiled with anger. She'd not gone through everything she'd gone through in these mountains, simply to hand the ring over so easily. "So you'd leave me and Abchar here, would you? What are we supposed to do, walk all the way back to Ring Isle now we've done the hard bit?"

"Hard bit?" Neesha planted her hands on her hips and glared at Tilda. "What have you done that's been hard? We've looked after you every step of the way. All you did was a bit of digging at the end—"

"And who had to keep sticking her hand into freezing water?" Tilda stepped forward until her nose almost touched Neesha's. "Who was it that you depended on to say if we'd gone far enough up the river? Who almost got killed by an ox—"

"Quiet." Abchar forced the girls apart with his meaty hands. "Give Abchar the message."

"But it's mine and—"

"Give!" Abchar's tone did not encourage further argument. Neesha gave, reluctantly, and then glared at Tilda as though it was all her fault, while Abchar read what Silviu had written.

"We all go back," Abchar said eventually. "Together. Say all names where it says Neesha."

"Do you think that'll work?" Tilda chewed her lip. Of course she wanted to go back, but what if the enchantment wasn't strong enough to take three of them to Silviu? Would it select just Neesha, leaving Tilda on the mountainside with Abchar? Would something terrible happen to all three of them? They might be hurt or—

Abchar grunted again. "Maybe. Maybe not."

"Well, don't blame me if it all goes wrong," Neesha snapped, tears sparkling in her eyes. "It was your decision, Abchar, not mine. So you can explain to my father why it took weeks to get back to him instead of moments. When . . . if . . . we see him." She held out her hand again. "Give me the parchment. We're wasting time."

"Hold hands." Abchar held one hand out to Neesha. "We not get separated." Only when she took it did he give her the slip of parchment he still held in the other hand.

Tilda grabbed that other hand before Neesha could even open her mouth. She was not under any illusion that if Neesha could, she'd leave her behind . . .

"Ready?" Abchar looked down at Tilda, then at Neesha.

Tilda nodded, her stomach full of fluttering butterflies. What would it be like this time, to travel over such a great distance? There was no book to be sucked into, just that tiny slip of parchment— and she doubted very much that it was big enough to suck *her* up, let alone another two people, and one of those a giant. Would they come out crushed at the other end? Suddenly, it didn't seem like a very good idea at all to try to say all three names, even if *was* going to get the ring back to Silviu. She shoved her hand into her pocket and held onto the ring tightly. Well, if the worst came to the worst, and only Neesha got back, then—

Neesha began to speak. "Threshnar—"

"Wait!" Tilda shouted. "The ring! If this enchantment does only work for you, then you need to hold onto it. Otherwise, you might end up trapped on Ring Isle like everyone else, but without the ring and no way to help Silviu."

"She right."

Reluctantly, Tilda pulled her hand and the ring out of her pocket and offered the silviron circle to Neesha.

"I'll take good care of it." Neesha took it from her. "I promise. And thank you."

Tilda nodded, trying not to mind. It made sense to hand the ring over, especially if the enchantment did only work for Neesha, but it didn't stop her feeling a twinge of envy as the precious object disappeared into someone else's pocket.

"Shall we try again?" Neesha took a deep breath and recited the strange words for the second time. "Threshnar braythnay kristallmett. Retornath ab Neesha, Tilda, Abchar almaynar heralma."

For a second, Tilda thought nothing was going to happen.

Then the air around their feet began to swirl silently, rising faster and higher until all three of them were trapped inside a mini-whirlwind.

"Hold tight!" Abchar yelled.

All the breath was sucked out of Tilda's body as the air roared and something vast and powerful latched onto her and pulled. Everything went black, and she heard Neesha scream. Tilda couldn't blame her. The darkness was absolute; she couldn't see anything—not even her hand in front of her face.

She could only feel . . . Everything in her world became swirling air and roaring wind and blackness, apart from the roughness of Abchar's hand, crushing hers, the stinging of cheeks whipped by loose hair, and the tightness of her chest as she fought to catch a breath.

And then, slowly, so slowly Tilda wasn't sure if she was imagining it at first, the darkness began to lift. First, there were outlines, then faint hints of detail, and finally, there was Abchar. And, thank Power, Neesha, gripping Abchar's arm with both hands, eyes squeezed shut and face pale. Ruby light poured from her pocket, colouring the walls of their airy prison a dull, deep red.

How long did it last? Tilda had no idea. But eventually, the air slowed and settled, showing dim shapes beyond the thinning walls of the whirlwind. A brighter square—was that a window? A dark shadow—could that be a chair? The glow from Neesha's pocket seemed to grow and intensify, until redness coloured everything within and without the whirlwind.

As the air's movement faded to little more than a whisper around Tilda, she looked down. She was standing on a wine coloured carpet. When she looked up, her heart gave a great leap of joy. Silviu's bed! Silviu's desk! And over there . . . She frowned when she saw the old man sitting in the tree trunk chair.

"We're on Ring Isle," Neesha whispered.

The man rose stiffly to his feet.

"Thank the Power. Yes, you are," Silviu croaked.

Chapter 22
An Unwelcome Return

HOW COULD SILVIU have changed so much? He'd slumped back into the tree trunk chair, a shadow of the man Tilda had last seen only a few days before. His eyes had lost their brightness, his hands were like claws where they gripped the arms of his seat, and fresh lines had added years to his face.

"Neesha . . ." Silviu raised a shaking hand. "Is it really you?"

"It's me," Neesha said, kneeling beside his chair as Silviu stroked her hair. "Pa, you look awful."

"I am weary and drained of Power. As a result, I'm not looking my best." He tried to smile. "I used too much creating a doorway to leave"—his eyes flicked briefly in Tilda's direction—"so thank Power I enchanted your locket a long time ago, so you could come straight to me if you were in danger. I didn't expect it to be strong enough to bring more than one of you back, though Power knows I am pleased to see you and Abchar." He reached out to the giant, standing on the other side of his chair, and clasped his forearm. "We need his strength."

"Abchar will do what he can," Abchar growled.

Tilda swallowed hard. Was Silviu pleased to see her, too, after what she'd done? "My Lord . . ." She would've stepped closer to the huge chair, but her courage failed when Silviu fixed her in that familiar ice blue gaze. Her mouth went dry, and she licked her lips before she could continue. "I'm . . . I'm sorry I went through the book instead of you. I didn't mean to."

"Look, Pa—we found the ring." Neesha dug deep in her pocket and pulled out the silviron circle. It glowed gently between her fingers.

"Ahhh." Silviu leant back against the chair, closed his eyes, and breathed a great sigh. "The Power can return," he murmured. "Your ability to see the auras came in handy then, Tilda?"

If he'd leapt out of his chair and thumped her in the chest, Tilda couldn't have been more winded. Her mouth opened and closed several times before she managed to say, "You knew?"

Silviu opened his eyes and sat a little straighter in the chair. "I knew as soon as you walked into the Ring Room that you could feel the Power—some people can, though they are rare. Rarer still are those who can see the auras, which you demonstrated when you said . . . something about understanding how the regions got their colours."

Yes, she had said that, hadn't she?

"I would have known, even if you had not said anything. The auras were reflected in your eyes." Silviu paused, as though remembering the moment. Then he leaned forward. "And that's why I used you."

Used her—what was she, a tool?

"When Yaduvir isolated us all, I knew it could not be me who left Ring Isle. The other mages would have been too weak, too devoid of Power, to contain him. I needed someone else to go, and your ability to both see and feel the Power you hated so much—"

Tilda's cheeks burned. "I didn't hate it, I was angry about how the Power had been—"

Silviu held up a hand. "—were essential, especially as you wouldn't be missed. And with help, you found the ring and brought it back."

She stared at him in disbelief. He really *had* used her, hadn't he? Why hadn't he told her anything of what he had planned to do? She understood the danger which faced Issraya with no access to the Power. She'd have done whatever she could to help get the ring back, but it would've been nicer to have been asked, to have been given the choice and an explanation. Then at least she wouldn't have had the shock of landing in Ambak with no idea of what was going on.

"Nearly didn't," Abchar rumbled.

"Didn't what?" Silviu said. "Find the ring, or get back?"

"Both," Neesha told him.

Silviu frowned. "Why? What happened?"

"Yaduvir," Tilda said.

Silviu's eyes narrowed. "What? How?"

"He'd magicked your snake torc." Tilda rubbed her wrist, remembering how its coils had crushed her bones. "Was watching through its eyes and saw me find the ring. He appeared on the mountain, tried to take it."

"My snake torc?" Silviu frowned. "But I'd put it into my pencil box, on the…" He paused. "Tilda. Did you take it?"

She nodded and the words tripped off her tongue as she tried to explain. "I didn't mean to. I was tidying up, couldn't put your pencils away, so I put it in my pocket to ask you where it should go, but the books fell and you told me to leave and I didn't have a chance to ask and—"

"Then Yaduvir knows the ring is here, you stupid girl," Silviu hissed, pointing at her. Red sparks fizzed at the end of his finger, growing stronger, brighter.

Abchar grabbed Neesha and pulled her behind him.

"No, no, no! He won't!" Tilda raised a hand in front of her face as though that would be enough to ward off a fireball. "The eagle you'd made attacked Yaduvir, destroyed the torc. He can't know anything that's happened since then."

"Pa, it's true!" Neesha shouted, trying in vain to get round Abchar. "What's left of that torc is still in the mountains."

With a faint pop, the sparks disappeared and Silviu allowed his hand to fall into his lap. "Then there's still a chance . . . Neesha, give me the ring."

And that was it? No apology? Anger tightened Tilda's chest, making it hard to breathe. The Power really was all that he was concerned about, wasn't it? He didn't want to know that she'd faced terrible weather and wild animal attacks *and* a rogue powermage in the hunt for the ring that *he'd* deliberately lost.

As soon as the ring made contact with Silviu's palm, the red glow pulsed and grew around his hand, spreading further until his arm was enveloped up to the elbow. Was it Tilda's imagination, or did he look less tired already? There was a little more colour in his face, the worry lines seemed to be fading . . . Then she remembered how the ache in her own ankle had disappeared when she touched the Power under the Ambak bush, back at the pool where she found the ring. She couldn't begrudge him some pain relief.

"Ah, that's better." Silviu sighed, laying the ring down on the arm of his chair. "I shouldn't draw too much. Yaduvir will become suspicious of my sudden recovery. The ring really needs reinstalling in the Ringstone so I can recharge properly."

"Then what are we waiting for?" Neesha said. "Let's do it. Now!"

Silviu shook his head. "It's not that simple. Yaduvir is planning to destroy the Ringstone."

"What? No—he can't!" Tilda gasped, surprising herself. She might not like how Silviu used the Power sometimes, but for Issraya's mages to be unable to draw on it at all . . . That didn't bear thinking about.

"Oh, but he can. Duska, Taimane, Kamen, and myself are drained of Power, while he remains full of dark magic, magic which allowed him to break loose of our restraints and confine us to our rooms until we are called upon to witness the destruction. Yaduvir intends to rule Issraya without the Power we have relied on for millennia." He touched the ring gently, and it flared red. "I have devised a plan in the hope that the ring was returned in time, and—"

The bedroom door suddenly opened.

Abchar leapt at the man who'd opened it, and they both crashed to the ground. Everyone shouted at once.

"No!"

"Let him go!"

"Uncle Vanya!"

"Huh?" Abchar looked confused, then recognition dawned on his face. He jumped up and hauled a dishevelled Vanya to his feet. "Abchar apologise."

Vanya looked completely dazed. "Abchar? But I thought you were—Neesha? How are you—?" His eyes flicked between them, and then fell on . . . "Tilda?" He took two swift strides and caught her up in a crushing hug. "Tilda," he whispered hoarsely. "We couldn't find you, I thought . . ."

Tilda's attempt at a reply was muffled against his chest. She pulled away and tried again. "I'm alright, Uncle Vanya."

"Vanya, there will be time for explanations later." Silviu's voice had taken on a tone of authority. He pushed himself to his feet and held up the ring. "It has returned."

Vanya let Tilda go. His face set in an expression of determination. "So we can fight."

"Indeed. There isn't time to do anything now before Yaduvir's ceremony of destruction, but can you get a message to Taimane, Kamen, and Duska? Tell them to be prepared when we are summoned, and to wait for my signal in the Ring Room."

Vanya gave a curt nod. He spun on his heel, gave Tilda a tight smile, and was gone almost as quickly as he'd come.

Silviu turned to Abchar. "Abchar, if you can, draw together a fighting force from among the servants. I have no doubt that the door to the Ring Room will be barricaded to prevent any such interference, but you must do your best to break in."

Abchar's single eye glittered. "Abchar will do. Abchar like a good fight." He grinned and headed after Vanya.

"I don't have much time." Silviu gestured towards his wardrobe. "Tilda, fetch my initiation robe."

"What can I do?" Neesha asked.

"Nothing. You'll stay here, where you'll be safe."

Tilda pulled the robe from its hanger and cringed. Did Silviu really know so little about his own daughter, he'd tell her that? She hadn't known Neesha long herself, but even she could see that Neesha really wasn't the kind of person to play safe. She glanced over her shoulder.

Silviu was pacing up and down, muttering to himself. "I'll need a diversion when the time comes to put the ring back, and—"

"I'm not staying here," Neesha said, glaring at her father.

Silviu frowned at the interruption. "You will do as I tell you. This is not your battle."

"No. it's yours and the Power's, isn't it? Well, I hate the Power, hate it!"

"Neesha!" Red light flared around Silviu, and his eyes flashed as fiercely as his daughter's.

Neesha ignored him. "You always put the Power first, not me. You never let me share what you have to do for it, but she"—she flung an arm out towards Tilda—"is only a servant and you've involved her!"

"It wasn't exactly a choice—" Tilda began.

"Neesha, I'm warning you—"

"I hate it when you're away because the Power needs you to do something wonderful for someone." Neesha actually stamped her foot. "It's never for me, is it? I never get your attention, with or without the Power's prompting." Her voice dropped to a whisper and her shoulders slumped. "I may as well not have a father."

"But you do," Tilda snapped, without thinking, as a surge of anger burned inside her. "You do have a father. Be glad of it, because there are plenty who don't. Like me, because the mages wouldn't use the Power to help my Pa. So what if your Pa puts using the Power before being a father? At least he's not dead." She threw Silvu's robe down on the bed.

"You . . ." Silviu's lips pulled tight. He took a deep breath and spoke slowly and carefully, his whole body vibrating with anger. He took a step towards Tilda. "You assume too much, Matilda Benjasson. You dare to speak on matters of which you have no knowledge, and belittle the sacrifices I am forced to make?"

But she was too angry, too hurt as Pa's loss made itself felt afresh, to listen. "If you think being a powermage is so important, then use the Power properly! Not to make stitched animals move, or send fireballs at people's heads, or make doorways in books that suck people into the mountains without telling them. Use it to do what you're supposed to, and save Issraya!"

"What do you think I'm trying to do?" Silviu shouted at her.

The blood drained from Tilda's cheeks, leaving her cold. She gripped the bedpost to steady herself.

Silviu snatched up his robe. "What do you know about any of this, Tilda? After everything you've experienced, you're still just an ignorant servant girl with no real understanding of how the Power works to protect Issraya." He thrust his arms roughly into the sleeves and turned his back on her. "I expected better of you. Leave me. And don't come back."

Tears prickled Tilda's eyes. "So you don't need an ignorant servant girl any more, now she's brought you the ring back? Perhaps you can use your daughter instead. She's brave and strong and clever, might fit the bill better." Silviu did not respond, and Tilda's hands balled into fists. "D'you know what? Yaduvir's bad for using dark magic. But you're worse, because you use people." As soon as the words were out of her mouth, she regretted them.

"Tilda!" Neesha's eyes were wide with shock, and she looked quickly at her father.

Slowly, Silviu turned. In his hand was a red ball of light. "Get. Out. Now," he growled.

As the fireball shot towards her, Tilda ducked; it exploded against the door jamb.

She ran out of his rooms as fast as she could and then limped along deserted corridors with tears streaming down her face and her breath coming in sobbing gasps.

Why had she ever agreed to come to Ring Isle? She should've fought harder to stay at home with Ma. That way, neither she or Silviu would ever have found out that she could see and feel the Power, he wouldn't have decided to send her through the doorway, she wouldn't have had to face the oxala or the blizzard or Yaduvir . . .

She stopped to rest and leaned against the wall to catch her breath, but her thoughts ran on without stopping.

After all she'd gone through, how could Silviu turn the Power against her like he had? She was pretty certain the Power wasn't meant to be used to make fireballs, especially when those fireballs were then thrown at people who were telling the truth about mages who sometimes used the Power in ways that didn't help the people of Issraya.

Actually, now she thought about it, Tilda had only seen Silviu do that. She had no evidence at all against Kamen, Duska, and Taimane. Perhaps she shouldn't tar them with the same brush, should find out more about how they approached their responsibilities. See if Silviu was the exception, rather than the rule . . .

"No," she muttered, pushing herself away from the wall and limping on. She wasn't going to hang around long enough to find that out. As soon as the mages had beaten Yaduvir and broken through his isolation enchantment, she'd be off. Back to Merjan City and Ma, no matter what Uncle Vanya or Aunt Tresa said. She'd had her fill of Power and mages.

Almost as though thinking about the Power had drawn her close to it, Tilda found herself outside the Ring Room doors, and her footsteps slowed.

When she first arrived on Ring Isle, she'd been angry with the Power *and* the mages. Hated both of them for letting Pa die, for forcing Ma to sell everything to pay for useless medicine, and because the situation had forced Tilda to leave home, live with relative strangers, and be close to the very thing she held responsible for Pa dying.

But right now, at this moment, there was really only one place where her anger was directed; Silviu.

Yes, she was angry with Silviu. But angry at the Power? Not any more . . . She'd seen it, felt it. Touched it. That the Power was real, she could not deny. But she was beginning to wonder whether the Power had any say in how it was used. Or whether its use was entirely down to the decisions made by the mages.

Slowly, Tilda passed the Ring Room doors. Silviu had made decisions to protect the Power—hadn't she experienced them, firsthand, at the failed initiation—and he had also attempted to put things right, even if he had used Tilda in the process. And from what he'd said since her return, he was planning to work together with the other mages to replace the ring, restore their access to the Power, and then use it to prevent Yaduvir from inflicting further harm on Issraya.

If Silviu's new plan succeeded, was it proof enough for Tilda that he did, ultimately, have the protection of Issraya as a priority, regardless of how else she'd seen him use the Power? Could she forgive him for mis-using the Power in trivial ways if the safety of Ma, Uncle Vanya, Aunt Tresa, Captain Abram, Neesha and Abchar and Stefan and Marja and everyone else she knew and loved and every single person living in Issraya could be secured?

Perhaps, if she witnessed Silviu actually using the Power to overcome and subdue someone as terrible as Yaduvir, maybe it wouldn't hurt so much every time she thought about Pa afterwards, knowing that although he'd died, so many other people *had* been saved.

Almost without thinking, Tilda tried the handle of the door to the Ring Room's balcony. It was still unlocked. On silent feet, she sped up the stairs. Up on the balcony, she peered over the rail and looked down. The Ring Room was empty, the shadows of clouds crossing the mosaic floor in between bursts of sunshine.

Tilda sat herself down and leaned against the wall. As she made herself comfortable, her heart beat a rapid tattoo against her ribs, the blood rushed through her veins, and fluttering, fang-toothed butterflies filled her stomach. All she could do now was wait and watch the storm clouds gathering beyond the glass ceiling, trying not to think about all the terrible things Yaduvir might do to her homeland if Silviu and the other mages couldn't defeat him.

Chapter 23

Fighting Back

WHEN THE DOORS to the Ring Room finally crashed open, it took Tilda a few moments to persuade her stiff muscles to respond. When they did, she crawled to the balcony edge and slowly lifted her head above the rail.

Yaduvir was standing below, dressed in his shimmering, shifting wave-robe. He clapped his hands and said, "traymanth luminia!" At his command, several glowing balls of light appeared, suspended in mid-air and casting a pale illumination on the people following him into the storm-darkened room.

Tilda pressed a hand to her mouth to stifle her cry of surprise.

The rest of the mages were all in their robes, too, but they did not look so impressive now; Duska had lost none of her grace, but her hair hung lank and uncombed around her face and one arm was in a sling. Kamen shuffled slowly behind her, a bloodstained bandage wrapped around his bald head. Taimane's limp was nothing unusual, but a fresh black eye which almost matched the colour of his purple cloak, was. Only Silviu was visibly uninjured, though his face still bore the signs of exhaustion. He walked slowly but proudly, the last of the mages, his hands buried in the folds of his robe.

What had Yaduvir done to them all?

The stewards came in too, free of injuries but wary and watchful. Tilda bit her lip when she saw her uncle's dark head beside Freyda's blonde one.

A flick of Yaduvir's wrist, and there was a resounding crash as the doors slammed shut, sealing everyone inside.

"And here we all are in the Ring Room"—his voice rose up to Tilda on the balcony, just like it had during the initiation—"though it won't be that for much longer of course. Now, I don't want anyone to miss a moment of what I have planned, so take to your colours. It's the last time they'll have any meaning for you and the people of Issraya."

"You won't get away with this," Taimane snarled.

"Oh, I think I might." Yaduvir clicked his fingers.

Taimane's head snapped back as though from an invisible blow. Duska's cry masked Tilda's own horrified gasp.

"My lady Duska, your concern does you credit, but see? He is not harmed badly," Yaduvir said. "Why, there's hardly even any blood."

Tilda watched Taimane wipe a trickle of red from the corner of his mouth.

"Now, where were we? Oh yes—to your colours. No, no, no!"

Kamen and Duska had taken several steps towards the Ringstone and now stopped, obviously confused.

"Over there, at the sharp ends." As the mages and stewards moved into position on the points of the star, Yaduvir went in the opposite direction. He stared down at the Ringstone. "This ugly rock is useless without a full complement of rings. I really think that removing it is the way forward . . ." He trailed long fingers over the flat top, making circles in the empty space where the Ambakian ring should have been. Suddenly, his head snapped up, black eyes glittering. "None of you can stop me. You are powerless. I, on the other hand, am not, thanks to darker magics." He laughed, softly. "I am going to smash this stone to pieces."

This was the moment to act, surely? Tilda gripped the edge of the balcony, watching for Silviu's signal.

He gave none. Instead, he said, "You could always keep it whole."

"Oh?" In six long strides, Yaduvir stood in front of Silviu, the end of his nose only an inch away from the mage's face.

Silviu did not even blink.

"Pray tell," Yaduvir said, every syllable of his speech dropping into a silence so thick, you could almost cut it, "how keeping this relic in one piece would be of benefit to me?"

"Because we assumed you would prefer to have something to gloat over, you despicable little man," Duska spat at him.

Yaduvir spun towards her, hissing.

"Now, Neesha!" Silviu yelled. His hand shot out from the folds of his robe and threw something which flashed, silvery grey, as it flew through the air.

At the same moment, Neesha leapt from the darkness under the balcony.

"Breyknar immobilo!" Yaduvir screamed as his fist swung in a wide arc. It connected—hard—with Silviu's chin, slamming him back into one of the stone pillars.

The world and everything in it—including Tilda—froze. The only thing that continued to move was the ring, twisting and turning in mid-air, a mere hands-breadth from Neesha's outstretched fingers.

Yaduvir breathed a heavy sigh. "You dared to try to outwit me? Even now?" He shook his head. "Brave, but foolish."

Unable to move, her breath coming in shallow pants, Tilda could only watch as Yaduvir moved towards the ring. As though he were picking a flower, he plucked it out of the air and grinned, a smile more sinister and showing more teeth than any of the animal heads mounted in Silviu's room.

"Treynak remobilo."

The magical binding on Tilda's limbs was released, and her body sagged. She clung to the balcony rail to stay upright, her legs too weak to take her weight.

Neesha's leap continued. She crashed to the floor a short distance beyond Yaduvir's feet, her eyes wide and fearful in the pale orb-light.

"How touching—a family reunion. And all the sweeter because you brought the ring. Feel free to join your father, child . . ." Yaduvir made a sweeping gesture towards Silviu.

Neesha scrambled to her feet and scurried across the mosaic tiles until she reached her father and dropped to the floor beside him. Silviu stirred weakly, pulled her close, and enveloped her in the crumpled folds of his robe as though that would keep her safe.

No one on Issraya was safe, not now. Yaduvir had the ring.

Bile rose up in Tilda's throat and she swallowed it down.

"So how did you get back here, Neeee-sha?" Yaduvir tossed the ring into the air and caught it. "The torc was useless after its little run-in with that feathered fleabag, so I shall have to give the matter some consideration. Hmm . . ." He made a show of pretending to think, then clicked his fingers; Taimane winced at the gesture. "I bet your father had more Power left than I thought after our little altercation at my initiation. Enough to manage another enchantment, am I right?"

Neesha must have shaken her head.

"No? Well, however it was managed, there was obviously enough Power to transport you, his darling daughter, to safety." He tutted and shook his head. "So predictable, Silviu. And such a shame, you wasted all that Power. Because you've failed, you know." He strode quickly to where Silviu still lay, crumpled, at the foot of the pillar, and bent over him. "Look at you, nothing but a shell. And all for what? Not this, surely?" Yaduvir thrust the silviron circle under Silviu's nose, before straightening abruptly. "I'm glad you stopped me from destroying the Ringstone. Not, as the Lady Duska seems to think, because I need a trophy, but because now, the ring can be reinstalled. I shall fill myself with the Power to supplement the dark magic already in my possession, and rule Issraya."

No. No, this could not be happening. Tilda dug her nails into her palms as Yaduvir moved back towards the Ringstone. Surely Silviu would do something? She willed him to get up, to use whatever Power he still had, anything to stop Yaduvir! But all he did was hug Neesha closer. She looked at the other mages, willing them to act, but they looked utterly defeated.

No one was going to do *anything*?

A movement caught Tilda's eye; Freyda had stepped forward. She stood alone on the blue tiles of Merjan, a curious expression on her face that Tilda could not identify. "I don't think so, Yaduvir."

"What!" Yaduvir spun round.

Freyda smiled. "I think I'll take Issraya for myself." Her outline shivered.

Tilda's stomach lurched. She'd seen that happen once before.

"Extellembrath moratta!" Yaduvir yelled, and a ball of blue fire shot from his hand and sped towards Freyda.

"Extinguay," she shouted, and the fire winked out.

Freyda had magic? How was that possible? And yet, as Tilda continued to watch, a dark aura emerged around the steward. It coloured the air like a bruise, purple and black. Whatever was causing that aura, it was not warm and welcoming like the red light of the recovered ring. As it developed, Tilda's body grew heavy and listless. Her skin prickled and itched, as though a million ants crawled across it; she wanted to scrape and scratch to rid herself of the feeling.

Down below, Freyda took another step closer to Yaduvir.

"What in all power is happ—"

Taimane's words were cut short by a complicated twist of Freyda's fingers, which left him open-mouthed and mute.

"I will have silence," she said.

Yaduvir's face had paled. He took a step back and muttered under his breath, twisting and turning and stretching black strands which had appeared between his agitated fingers.

Freyda took another step towards him.

"Shadarthred capturi!" Yaduvir yelled and tossed the bundle of black lines at her; they spread upwards and outwards in mid-air, like a net.

Freyda swatted the lines aside as though they were nothing, and the net collapsed into a puddle of black liquid at her feet. She stepped over it and continued to advance. "Huh! Shadow threads? Is that the best you can offer of all you were taught?"

Yaduvir took another step back. "Mortivariuth mustartrath!" Six golden knives appeared out of nowhere in front of him. They hovered at shoulder height, their points aimed at the steward. The command "Vrathkarth Freyda!" sent the knives shooting towards Freyda's head so fast, they left golden streaks in the air.

"Zentarn sheld," she said.

The knives shuddered to a halt at the outer edge of Freyda's dark aura, quivering as though they had slammed into an invisible wall. Then they fell, clattering, to the floor.

"Better, Yaduvir, better." Freyda smiled. "But not good enough. What a shame . . . that was the best of the weapons at your disposal."

Yaduvir took another step away from her, stumbling when his heel caught on the Ringstone. He grabbed it to save himself from falling. "How do you know that?"

"Because *I* taught you."

The floating orb-lights flickered, and Tilda experienced a sense of foreboding so strong, she retched. Oh, Power, no . . .

Something was happening to Freyda. Her outline was blurring within the darkness, her body melting and reforming as bright light writhed and twisted around her limbs. When she finally came back into focus, Freyda's transformation was complete. Pale eyes, glowing in the depths of dark sockets, glared out of a stranger's face. Thin black lips were drawn back in a snarl. Hair had thinned, leaving only straggling white wisps. Clawed hands, with nails like talons, ripped Freyda's blue surcoat to shreds and scattered the scraps around the person who now stood in her place, revealing skin threaded with wrinkles and furrowed with creases, but alive with patterns of dancing light which swirled and writhed like animated tattoos.

Who—what—was this? Tilda retched again as the dark aura swirled thickly, hiding the stranger. When it settled, the woman was clothed entirely in white; white leggings, white boots and a white sleeveless tunic. Everything about her—apart from her aura— radiated light so brilliant, Tilda was forced to squint.

"Mistress!" Yaduvir dropped to his knees, his eyes almost starting out of his head.

"It feels so much better to be back in my own skin." The shining woman stretched and laughed, setting lines of light dancing across her bare arms. "It has been a long time." She walked slowly around the Ringstone, taking in the other mages still standing on their coloured tiles. "None of you recognise me? For shame, I thought you would remember. It's only been fifteen years."

"Luisa," Silviu croaked.

The woman inclined her head towards him, and a wide strip of light appeared to slide down her cheek. "The very same. I'm glad I have not been entirely forgotten."

Luisa? Tilda had heard that name before. Of course! The woman who might have been the Ambakian powermage instead of Silviu. But why had she disguised herself as Yaduvir's steward? And why, if he had been her master, was Yaduvir calling her mistress?

"Mistress, forgive me," Yaduvir gabbled. "Had I known it was you, I would never have raised a hand against you."

"Oh, Yaduvir." The woman that was Freyda-Luisa sighed. "Get up. You make the place look untidy when you're grovelling. Look, the other mages manage to stand before me, why can't you?"

Tilda saw that it was true—even Silviu had managed to climb to his feet, though he was leaning heavily on Neesha's shoulder. His lips were moving, no doubt whispering assurances to his daughter.

Yaduvir chose to remain on his knees.

"What is it you hope to gain, Luisa?" Kamen's voice sounded hoarse. He cleared his throat loudly. "You had your chance all those years ago and were not chosen. Why come back now?"

"The Power made the wrong choice. It is I who should have been initiated mage of Ambak. Not Silviu," Luisa replied. "I have spent the years since that time looking for ways to take the Power which should have been mine. I now have enough alternate sources of magic to achieve that."

"How? The Power belongs to the people of Issraya, it can only be drawn by powermages," Duska said, frowning. "And you are not a powermage."

Luisa's outline shivered, and suddenly she was not beside the Ringstone any more but standing right in front of Duska, her hand raised.

Duska gasped and pulled her head back sharply.

Luisa ran an index finger down Duska's cheek, making the mage shudder. "No, My lady. I am not. But I shall still draw on it and it will belong to me," she said softly. "No thanks to *you*," she spat, spinning round and pointing at Yaduvir. "You failed me."

"I did my best," Yaduvir whined. "It wasn't my fault. I can explain—"

Luisa fixed him with a pale stare. "You forget, Yaduvir. I need no explanation. I know exactly what happened because I have been beside you throughout this debacle, in the guise of Freyda. I taught you so many of my arts and yet you did not complete the task I assigned. You weren't focused enough at the initiation. You allowed another's incantation to tear the rings apart and thwart my ambition." Her voice had risen to a shout and the patterns on her skin writhed in response, shining brightly against the purple-black.

Tilda shielded her eyes from the almost unbearable light, but could not stop watching.

Luisa's dark aura throbbed as she walked towards Yaduvir. "Don't forget, I also witnessed first hand that with the missing ring in your possession, you intended to take all of Issraya's Power for yourself. Did you really think that I would allow a specimen like yourself to hold this land for your own?"

"Mistress, please . . . I did not know . . . if only I'd known . . ." Yaduvir was grovelling. Tilda almost felt sorry for him.

"It's too late, Yaduvir," Luisa whispered, leaning over him. "You are of no further use." She straightened up abruptly and turned her back on him. "Ebonymat morbidius."

"No! Wait, please!" Yaduvir leapt up. Then he looked down in surprise at the dark and viscous mass that had appeared and wrapped itself around his feet.

The mass expanded rapidly. It looked like tar as it swarmed up Yaduvir's legs, reaching long thick fingers of black towards his waist. He flailed uselessly at the thing that was engulfing him, his pleas for mercy growing shriller when a rope of black snapped itself around one of his arms, pinning it to his side. His free hand beat at the blackness until it too was captured.

Tilda could feel the dark magic working. It tugged and pulled at her, hard and cruel, bringing to mind all the hurt and pain she'd ever experienced. She gritted her teeth against the scream which was threatening to escape and give her hiding place away.

Although if she had screamed, no one would have heard; Yaduvir was screaming too.

The black stuff was relentless. Slim tendrils spread over his chin and Yaduvir thrashed his head from side to side in an attempt to escape them, but they sealed his lips, silencing him. Moments later, he was completely enveloped in a black bubble, its walls distorting as he continued his desperate attempts to break free from within. Slowly, the bubble grew still. It looked like the shadow of a tall thin man, standing beside the Ringstone.

Then the bubble burst.

The blackness peeled itself open from the top down, and Tilda shook uncontrollably. There was no one—in fact, there was absolutely nothing—inside. Yaduvir had disappeared. All that remained of him was a circle of black goo on the tiled floor.

Yaduvir was gone. Dead, killed by the dark magic which Luisa commanded. How could the rest of the mages ever stand against her? One glance in their direction, one look at their faces and Tilda could see that they knew. They knew they could do nothing to stop Luisa.

What hope was there for the people of Issraya, now?

"Time to put the ring back, I think." Luisa bent over the black puddle, reached into it, and pulled out the silviron circle. She held it up in triumph, the metallic particles flashing as they reflected the light from her skin.

"Don't!" Taimane limped forward. "Luisa, this is not how it is supposed to be. You cannot take on the Power and rule Issraya alone. We know from history it doesn't work. The burden of powerbearing must be shared—it has been so since the first mages. It is not possible for a single person to wield the Power without dire consequences."

"Spare me the lecture, old man. In case you hadn't noticed, I have other magic at my command. It will harness Issraya's paltry stuff."

Luisa's blackened lips curved into a smile. "Finally, I will receive what should have been mine, and it will be you, and you and you and you," she jabbed a finger towards each mage in turn, "who experience rejection. Watch as I take it all from you."

This was the end, then. The end of Issraya. The end of the Power. Tilda's vision blurred but she blinked the tears away as Luisa, still smiling that terrible smile, dropped the ring back into the space waiting for it in the Ringstone.

Except she couldn't have done it properly, because the ring fell out; Tilda heard the tinkle as it landed on the tiled floor.

Luisa growled and the patterns on her skin flared white. She picked up the ring and tried again.

This time, Tilda saw the ring jump up, out of the hole it was supposed to fit. It was almost as though the ring did not want to be returned, or the Ringstone had spat it out. Was Luisa going to force it in, using dark magic?

On her third attempt, Luisa pushed the ring into the hole and laid her hand flat over it, her skin now almost blindingly white from the patterns swirling over it. When she slowly drew her hand away, it seemed that she had won—the ring was back where it should be.

"You see?" she gloated. "Nothing can stand against me. The circle is complete and—"

The ring leapt out of the stone, shot past Luisa's head, and landed somewhere underneath the balcony where Tilda was standing.

Silviu's face wore an expression of grim satisfaction.

Luisa spun towards him. She bore down on him like an avenging angel, her purple-black aura trailing behind like wings, the lines of light on her skin converging in her face and filling it with dazzling light.

"What did you do?" she yelled into Silviu's face.

He didn't answer, just drew himself up straighter.

"Tell me! Rentracta absolute."

From her vantage point on the balcony, Tilda saw the exact moment when the enchantment worked; Silviu's face went curiously blank. Don't tell her, she willed him. Don't tell her!

But already Silviu's mouth was moving, his throat straining against the words Luisa was forcing him to speak. "The last . . . of my Power . . . simple protection."

"Simple? Tell me," Luisa growled. "Restamanta vocalistay."

Silviu's shoulders slumped. "The one who recovered it must replace it."

As soon as he'd spoken, Tilda's legs gave way. She collapsed to her hands and knees, the noise of Luisa's laughter and the shouts of mages and stewards almost completely drowned out by the sound of blood pounding in her ears. She retched as a potent mix of anger and fear swirled around in her stomach, and she shook her head.

Silviu had done it again—used her without asking in his eagerness to protect the Power and make things complicated for Luisa. Hysterical giggles tickled the back of Tilda's throat. What was Silviu expecting her to do, for Power's sake? He'd seen what Luisa was capable of—yet he'd made it so that only Tilda could put the ring back and allow him a chance to stop the woman in her tracks. Perhaps Yaduvir's blow had addled Silviu's brain.

"Quiet!" Luisa shouted. "You?"

"No . . . I-I didn't . . . it wasn't me . . . I . . ." That was Neesha; she sounded terrified.

"Then who?"

Tilda shoved her fist into her mouth and bit on her knuckles, waiting to hear her own name spoken. Instead, a hugely magnified voice almost deafened her.

"Kratyamba obtayn finderruss," it boomed.

Tilda slapped her hands over her ears, gasping as a column of purple-blackness shot up above the balcony, heading towards the glass ceiling. At the end of the column was a giant hand, made of dark swirling cloud, its index finger pointing upwards and making circles in the air.

Suddenly, the finger stopped circling. It pointed. Straight at Tilda.

Before she could move, the hand caught her up. She screamed as she was lifted over the balcony's edge and held high above the

Ringstone. Seconds later, Tilda was dumped on the floor, close to Luisa. The cloud-hand disintegrated, and a real, flesh-and-blood hand replaced it, closing around Tilda's throat and lifting her up until her toes were only just kissing the tiled floor.

"Tilda?" Luisa peered into her face, pale eyes searching. "*You* found the ring? But how . . . ?"

Tilda choked, tried to pull in a breath, but Luisa's fingers were digging in too tight. There were stars in her vision, everything was turning grey. Then suddenly she was released and her feet hit the floor again. She bent double, gasping and coughing and massaging her neck.

"Retreevad," Luisa snapped.

There was the sound of something hard smacking into flesh, and Tilda winced. Who had been injured this time? Slowly, she stood, swallowing the rawness in her throat. Thankfully, no one appeared to have been hurt, so why couldn't she stop trembling?

Luisa stood an arms-length away from Tilda, the dark aura pulsing angrily. One of her hands was raised beside her ear, almost as though she had been about to swear an oath. Stuck to the palm of her open hand was the ring.

Luisa stretched out that hand. "Take it," she said, offering Tilda the ring.

She shook her head.

"Take it," Luisa whispered through gritted teeth.

Something inside Tilda clicked. The Power belonged to the whole of Issraya through the mages, not to Luisa. The mages would keep the peace, but she would bring chaos and ruin to the land. There was no way Tilda was going to give in to this woman and see the powermages defeated, see the Power misused. She'd rather die.

"No," she said, swallowing hard as Luisa's eyes narrowed and the light on her skin flared and settled into shifting patterns that made Tilda feel queasy.

"Exstreyth kadrak, livazda mortran," Luisa whispered.

Tilda gasped. She'd heard those words before. And just as she had had no control over her arm beside the pool on the mountainside then, here and now she had no control over her feet. Step by treacherous step, they walked her closer to Luisa.

Wisps of dark purple-black reached towards Tilda as Luisa continued to chant. "Kalamat libris unser, silviron internamusta."

It was such a simple thing to do, to take the ring and press it firmly into the hole where it belonged. Why was she fighting? She only had to take it from Luisa's hand, like so, and move to the Ringstone. See, there was the empty space, begging to be refilled.

Muffled shouts reached her, but the voices were tiny and what they said wasn't important. She ignored them, because all that remained was to drop the silviron circle into the hole, and—

A shower of silver sparks shot up from the stone. All five rings liquefied instantly, their glittering, molten silviron blending and mixing and running around the circle of circles until it was completely filled. They darkened as they solidified.

A shove sent Tilda crashing to the floor. She lay on the blue tiles of Merjan, dazed, but fully herself again.

Power. What had she done?

Tears sprang into her eyes. "I'm sorry," she whispered, though she didn't know who she was apologising to—the mages, the ring, or the people of Issraya.

Luisa circled the Ringstone, passing close to where Tilda lay. "I have waited fifteen years for this moment. Now, at last, I can begin." She stopped and stretched out her arms. "Initiatray vestimenti." Her body, so brilliant and white, turned black.

For a split second, Tilda thought the dark bubble which had devoured Yaduvir had returned. But then she blinked, and the reality swam into focus; Luisa had magicked a robe over her white clothes. Black as a raven's wing, it gleamed with green and purple and blue, a blackness somehow alive with sinister power. The light tattoos fell still in response, marking Luisa's face and hands with brilliant stripes.

Luisa gave a low chuckle and brought her outstretched arms together over the Ringstone. Then she lowered her hands onto the obelisk, covering all the rings at once. "Hastel athor, embarak nouray. Ilsteth horat umbaroth, clostardith verasta . . ."

The Power responded immediately. The five coloured flames of light shot out of the stone and started to climb up Luisa's arms. As they grew and surrounded her, the ever-present dark aura sucked them into itself, until it was shot through with flashes of blue and yellow, purple, red, and green.

Tilda could feel Issraya being sucked dry of Power as Luisa continued to chant and drain it from its source. How could words that were so beautiful and musical flood Tilda's body with such desolation and hopelessness?

Finally, the chant ended and thick, heavy silence filled the Ring Room.

"The strength!" Luisa gasped, throwing back her head. "It is incredible. I have magic *and* Power!" She laughed, pale eyes glittering. "Now to discover the full extent of my enhanced capabilities." Still laughing, she took a step away from the Ringstone. She would have taken a second, but was jerked back towards it; her hands had remained where they were, flat on the surface of the obelisk. The laughter died, replaced with a frown.

Tilda stared at Luisa. She was stuck—stuck to the Ringstone— and the coloured lights of the Power were still flooding into her. Oh, this was bad, very bad. Worse than when Yaduvir had tried to corrupt his own initiation ceremony. Because this time, there was no one to try and stop it from happening . . .

She had to move.

Quick as she could, Tilda shuffled backwards, aiming to put as much distance as she could between herself and the woman still standing at the obelisk. There was anger in the air, hot and fierce, pressing against her chest, making it hard to breathe. Would her ribs collapse under the weight of it? Gasping, she reached a pillar and leaned against it.

"Let go of me," Luisa growled, tugging and straining against whatever held her captive until the muscles of her arms cracked with the effort. The patterns of light on her skin moved in a dizzying dance. "Let go. Let go!"

The murmur of voices reached Tilda. She looked round and saw, under a neighbouring arch, the other mages standing shoulder to shoulder, their lips all moving in a synchronized chant.

Luisa must have heard them, too. "What are you doing? Stop it! Franstam prolifica, bronsamda relees!" Her words caused a shower of silver sparks to shoot up from the Ringstone, but she was not released. The purple-black aura was almost overwhelmed now by brighter shades and Luisa writhed and twisted, increasing her efforts to break free. The patterns of light on her skin darkened and wisps of smoke rose from her hands.

The stench of burning meat filled Tilda's nostrils. How much more Power could Luisa absorb before she was destroyed?

Luisa screamed something primitive and dreadful which hurt Tilda's ears to hear. Immediately, the coloured lights of the Power surged away from Luisa towards the Ringstone, dragging her dark aura with them.

With a snarl, Luisa finally broke free.

Five gigantic beams of coloured light shot straight up from the Ringstone, shattering the domed ceiling. Glass rained down; Luisa flung her arms up to protect herself. On her palms and fingers, smoking imprints of the circle of circles were visible; Luisa had been branded.

Stormy air was sucked into the room; the illumination orbs exploded, and everyone fought the wind to stay on their feet. There was a flash of lightning, a deafening crash of thunder, and heavy rain poured through the broken ceiling.

The beams had formed a tight coil of twisted, spinning light, which sucked the raindrops and wind into a swirling vortex around the Ringstone.

Tilda grabbed the nearest pillar and clung to it, eyes half-closed against the wind and rain and flashes of lightning. Above the thunder, she heard heavy pounding on the doors. Was that Abchar, trying to break in? If it was, he was too late–

The doors burst open. Abchar stood in the doorway, a crowd of black and grey uniformed staff at his back.

Even above the sound of the storm, Luisa's scream of frustration rang in Tilda's ears.

What little remained of Luisa's awful aura was being dragged from her by the strength of the wind. The light tattoos had faded, now dead and dark against the whiteness of her clothes. Luisa's face was contorted with rage, her eyes flashing.

"I have not finished with you, powermages of Issraya!" she screamed. "I will have this land yet! Dramathna uncene!"

Her outline shivered and she vanished.

Chapter 24
Making Contact

THERE WAS A moment of utter stillness, in spite of the raging storm and the twisting Power.

Silviu shattered it by shouting, "Mages, to your colours! Contain the Power!"

The storm sucked the air from Tilda's lungs and she could barely hear a thing above its terrible roar. What was happening? As her hair was whipped around her face, she buried her head into the crook of her arm to try to protect herself and still be able to see.

Abchar's makeshift army of servants were fighting to get closer, leaning into the wind with laboured steps.

The mages were also being buffeted by the wind as they headed towards the Ringstone. Finally they reached the golden tiles, their beautiful initiation robes soaked and bedraggled.

"Silviu, we can't!" Duska shouted, bracing herself against the Ringstone. Bathed in green light, her face took on a sickly shade. "There aren't enough of us."

"We might manage with four," Taimane yelled back.

"We must try—look!" Kamen pointed above their heads.

Tilda looked up too, half-blinded by falling raindrops. The five strands of light were as thick as ropes, twisting and coiling right up to and beyond the shattered glass dome. The Power wasn't supposed to do that! It was supposed to be drawn carefully out by the mages, not be set loose in huge quantities. Tilda was fully aware of its enormous potential in the tingling across every inch of her skin. How could that amount of energy ever be contained?

"Make contact," Silviu ordered. The red rope flared brightly at his touch, and his body went rigid.

Duska hesitated for only a second before there was a matching flare of green. Purple and yellow followed, proving that all four mages had connected with their rings.

"Please! Please let them be able to pull the Power back," Tilda whispered, clinging to the pillar.

Nothing happened. The strands of Power continued to spin and weave and coil together. It was stronger than the mages, it would all be lost. Issraya was doomed . . .

Or was it? Tilda stared hard; something *was* happening. Thank Power! Four of the colours were beginning to unwind themselves from the central mass, sinking back towards the rings which anchored them to the Ringstone. As though responding to the reduction in size of those columns, the blue one suddenly thickened, pulsing like an illuminated heartbeat.

"Draw more!" Taimane shouted.

"I can't!" Kamen shook his head.

"No more, please!" Duska pleaded.

"Do it!" Silviu threw his head back, face twisted with effort.

A low keening noise rose above the sound of the wind; Duska sounded like an animal in pain as she bent her head low over her hand. Purple sparks shot from the ends of Taimane's moustache.

Tilda looked up, blinking raindrops out of her eyes as she looked for any sign of change in the tower of blue light.

There was a change, but not the one she'd been hoping for; instead of getting smaller, the column appeared to be widening at its top. Oh Power, let her be wrong! But as she watched, the blue light started to spread out above the hole where the ceiling had once been, tinting the room below and everyone in it pale blue.

Tilda glanced across at where the mages were working together—and struggling. Four of them weren't enough. There needed to be five of them to stand any chance of bringing that blue strand under control, but no one else could see or feel what was happening.

Tilda's mouth fell open. Except her—she could do both. Should she . . . ? No. It had to be a powermage, someone chosen and initiated and . . .

Did it?

The thought of touching that blueness was terrifying. There was none of the gentle, warming redness she'd experienced when she'd connected with the Ambakian strand of Power. Even from a distance, she could tell this blue light was powerful, unstoppable. Like a storm tide crashing through the Merjan Straits . . . It would destroy her. The mages knew how to do this. They would succeed. They had to . . .

But what if they couldn't, and Tilda was the only other person able to help? Could she live with herself, knowing that she had a rare ability that might have made all the difference, but had chosen to do nothing? "I expected better of you," Silviu had said; was this the moment to show him the best she *could* give, even if it meant making the ultimate sacrifice for Issraya and its people?

Taimane noticed her approaching the Ringstone. "Get back!"

"No!" she yelled.

Duska raised her head with a huge effort. "You'll die!"

"I don't care!" The words sounded brave, but Tilda's heart stuttered as she pushed on against the wind. She might well be consumed by the Power or branded by the rings, but she had to try.

"Let her come," Silviu forced out through gritted teeth.

"Silviu, it's madness—"

"Only a mage—"

Tilda ignored the protests and stepped onto the golden tiles. There wasn't time to explain. She caught Silviu's eye. "Tell me what to do."

Silviu grimaced. "Touch the ring, coax the Power back."

Panic twisted Tilda's stomach into a knot when she felt her hand move; she was enchanted again, being forced to act against her will this time by Silviu. Then common sense kicked in—of course she wasn't. All the mages were concentrating so hard on trying to contain their portions of Power, a separate enchantment at the same time was beyond any of them. She'd moved her hand herself.

"Quickly!" Silviu gasped, as all the reduced strands expanded abruptly up to head height again.

The knot loosened a little in Tilda's stomach. She had to do this. Even if she died in the attempt. She held her breath and touched the ring from which the blue light was pouring.

Power surged through her body and left her breathless. Every nerve tingled and stung until she felt as though she'd fallen into a bed of nettles. Speak? To this? Where to begin? How did you address raw Power?

Feeling foolish, she began a conversation in her head.

Power! Too much . . . *Blue light?* Better . . . *Blue light, you must go back. Into the Ringstone.*

She felt, rather than heard, the voice which roared inside her head. It reminded her of storm waves crashing onto rocks.

Who is it that dares speak to the Power of Merjan?

In that instant, everything beyond the golden tiles on which Tilda stood slowed in time and fell silent. There was Abchar, running towards Neesha in slow motion. There were the servants behind him, pushing slowly into the room. And there were the raindrops, almost stationary in their descent, looking like floating diamonds.

Everything at the Ringstone remained normal. Was this happening because she'd spoken to the blue light? Or because the Power of Merjan had spoken to her?

Tilda swallowed hard. She ought to answer. "I'm Tilda . . . Tilda Benjasson."

The blueness intensified. It felt . . . angry.

Tilda Benjasson . . . you have not been initiated. How do you dare to speak to me?

How, indeed? Tilda forced herself to maintain contact with the ring, although every bit of her wanted to tear her hand away. She thought quickly. "Because I'm the only one who can, now Yaduvir's dead and—"

The column flared bright blue. *Yaduvir! That traitor!* it thundered in her head.

"He's dead!" she added quickly. "Luisa killed him."

Luisa . . . the Power seemed to sigh. *She tainted us with darkness, but we fought her.*

"You—what?"

The blue light jiggled and quivered. Was it laughing? *We left our mark on her.*

Tilda's eyes widened as she realised what the Power meant. "On her hands!"

Yessss . . . the admittance sounded like gentle waves soughing on a shingle beach. *She will find it harder to hide from us in future.* There was a moment of silence. *She has pulled me far from my anchor.*

It was true. The blue light was the only strand still outside the broken glass dome—the others had been drawn right back to the hands of their mages, who were all staring at Tilda, eyes wide.

"She has. But . . . can't you just . . . slide back? Like the other colours?"

The column flared. *Why should I? I am unbound and unfettered. Why should I return to the obelisk, to be trapped again with the ring as a key, until I am called upon to release some of myself?* The Power fizzed and buzzed through Tilda's body; it felt raw and alive. Almost . . . exhilarated.

Oh, this wasn't going well. Tilda racked her brain for something that would persuade the Power to comply. "It's too dangerous for you to be unbound like this. Most people can't survive being exposed to raw Power, that's why we need the powermages, because they can. It's only them who can draw you when they need you." Even if they didn't always use it right. Anger flared briefly in Tilda's chest at the thought of what Silviu had done with it.

The light twisting and turning above Tilda became marginally stiller. *You hold . . . anger . . . towards us.*

"Oh." She was going to have to be very, very careful how she phrased her next few words. "I *was* angry. Very angry. Because Pa died and you didn't save him, even though he always trusted you. I hated you for that." A flash of brilliant blue made her wince, and she hurried on. "But I blamed you unfairly. You can't decide how the mages use you, can you?"

No. We cannot. We exist to be used, like a tool, Tilda Benjasson.

Ahh . . . Now she knew how to coax the Power back. Tilda took a deep breath. "Pa always told me that the mages use you to protect the ordinary people of Issraya. How can you let everyone down, and put them in danger, when they need you?"

The blue light dimmed, and Tilda felt . . . guilt?

"I'm not doing this for me . . ."

Ahh . . .

". . . I'm doing it for the people of Issraya."

The light flared brightly again, but remained silent.

Tilda chewed her lip, waiting for the Power to speak. Had it taken offence because she'd said too much, pushed her luck? She trembled, wondering if these were to be her final moments alive.

Then the Power spoke. *You are an exceptional person, Tilda Benjasson, to remind me of my duty. You are right. I exist to serve the people of Issraya.* It paused. *I am yours to command.*

Tilda sagged with relief. "You are? Then will you come back down to the Ringstone? Please?"

I will.

The blueness shrank and dropped below the level of the broken ceiling for the first time. It passed through Tilda, the sensation akin to being doused in warm water, drawing back to Ringstone, until only a pulsing blue glow remained, bathing her hand with blue light. When it didn't completely disappear, like the other colours had, Tilda's heart beat wildly in panic. Had it changed its mind? Was it not going to do as she'd asked?

I think we shall meet again, Tilda Benjasson, the Power whispered, and the blue glow winked out.

Immediately, time sped up beyond the golden tiles; the wind howled, the rain fell, Abchar ran to Neesha, and the servants poured into the Ring Room.

"You did it," Taimane said, staring at Tilda as water dripped off his moustache.

Duska was crying, her tears mixing with raindrops. Kamen leaned, exhausted, against the Ringstone. Silviu was nodding.

"It talked to me," Tilda whispered. "I'm not going mad, am I?"

At that, Silviu's nod turned to a definite shake. "No, you're not mad, Tilda Benjasson. But you are very, very special."

Chapter 25
The Mage of Merjan

TILDA WAITED ALONE, pacing up and down the corridor, her stomach churning. The back of her neck prickled and she rubbed at it, but her palms were sweaty and that felt even worse. She wiped them down her new skirt.

If only she could have worn the black and grey uniform today. It was comfortable and practical, "but not the sort of thing worn on these occasions," Aunt Tresa had told her, firmly. What *was* suitable turned out to be a long black skirt with a sprinkling of tiny blue beads around the hem, and a plain white shirt.

Even though she'd been expecting it, Tilda jumped when the Ring Room doors opened. She stopped her pacing. This was it. She pulled her shoulders back and lifted her chin high. Then she stepped through the doors and walked under the balcony, her eyes fixed on the Ringstone and the silver haze dancing above it.

The mages were standing on their region's colours, waiting for her. They were all smiling, thank Power. There had been times over these last few days when Tilda had wondered if they'd ever stop frowning or asking questions, and agree to what was going to happen to her.

Duska looked beautiful, her auburn hair braided and tipped with green glass beads. Taimane's moustache had been heavily waxed for the occasion, curling so far back on itself, it almost pricked his nose. Kamen's face was even more wrinkled than usual as he beamed his pleasure. Silviu stood tall and proud, and tilted his head in acknowledgement when Tilda halted just under the edge of the balcony.

"We are gathered today to welcome our new powermage, Matilda of Merjan," he announced. "She is our person of choice and invited here to be initiated into the mystery of powerbearing."

Tilda knew exactly what was expected of her. So why were her feet suddenly so reluctant to walk her forward, towards her future? Was she really the mages' person of choice? Were they absolutely sure there was no one else they'd rather have as the mage of Merjan?

"Tilda?" Silviu beckoned her forward.

As she stepped out of the shadows, Tilda glanced upwards. The balcony was full to bursting, there were so many faces peering down at her. Some of them were new to her, others more familiar, and some were very much loved.

Right opposite her was Ma, her face flushed with pride; Tilda had felt foolish asking the Power for favourable winds to allow Ma to arrive in good time, but *Silver Fish* had apparently almost flown across the Inner Sea. Ma was dabbing at her eyes with a spotted handkerchief—hopefully they were happy tears—and Captain Abram, standing beside her, snaked an arm around her waist. A jolt ran through Tilda's body when Ma laid her head on Abram's shoulder, because the captain wasn't Pa. But he was far better than Baker Arnal. On Abram's other side stood Aunt Tresa, the dimples in her cheeks visible even from this distance, she was smiling so broadly. And behind those three was a figure Tilda had no difficulty in spotting; Abchar stood head and shoulders above everyone else, grinning his pirate's grin. There were only two other people she wanted to be sure were here—and they wouldn't be up on the balcony. As she had known he would be, Uncle Vanya was in position on the point of the red triangle, a rare smile on his face.

Tilda stopped in the exact same place on the blue tiles of Merjan where Yaduvir had stood not so long ago, fighting the urge to look down and check that every trace of that terrible black puddle had gone.

Was she dreaming? She pinched herself, hard, just to be sure; it hurt and she didn't wake up, so yes, this was really happening. She, Matilda Benjasson, had been chosen to be a powermage, the youngest in the history of Issraya. She still couldn't believe it, and was half expecting Silviu to tell her it had all been a joke, that they had actually lined up someone much older and wiser to be the next Merjanian mage . . . But he didn't, and Tilda's heart set up a hard banging against her ribs. For the first time today, she was glad of her long skirt; it hid her shaking legs.

"Do you, Matilda, agree to be used as a vessel for the Power, and swear to use that Power for the good of Issraya in the service of its land and people?" the mages asked in unison.

The whole room seemed to be holding its breath, waiting for Tilda's answer.

Now it had come to this moment, did she agree? She knew now that the Power had no choice in how it was used—that was up to her and the other mages to decide. Could she really make those tough decisions, even if it meant that some Issrayans turned against her for it, like she'd turned against Silviu for a while?

Yes, she could. Willing her legs to keep still, Tilda took a deep breath. "I do."

There was a movement behind her. Tilda knew who it was, but didn't turn round, even though she would have loved to watch Neesha approaching with the new initiation robe. Thank Power Silviu had eventually given in to her request that Neesha should fill the role of steward for this important ceremony. She had helped Tilda to find the lost ring, and deserved some sort of reward. A more permanent choice of steward could come later.

"How does it feel?" Neesha whispered, helping Tilda into the robe.

"Good," she whispered back.

And it did, even though it wasn't as fancy or ornate as the ones worn by the other mages, because everyone expected that Tilda would soon grow out of it. Aunt Tresa had still done a good job, stitching a flotilla of Inner Sea boats around the hem of a plain blue robe. Tilda had been delighted to find that one of them had a tiny silver fish at its prow. When she had stopped growing, she'd ask Tresa to make another robe. One which had a thick column of twisting blue light breaking out of the glass dome on top of a high tower . . .

She glanced up at the still broken ceiling as Neesha moved away. Thank Power the sun was shining today in a cloudless sky visible through the hole where the glass should have been. Today was not a day she wanted to be rained on.

She stepped onto the golden tiles; Silviu took her right hand, Duska her left, and they raised them high.

"Then we welcome you to our fellowship!" the mages cried.

Deafening applause broke out on the balcony. Duska placed a feather-light kiss on Tilda's cheek, the glass beads clinking gently against one another. Taimane slapped her on the back with one hand and tugged at his waxed moustache with the other. Kamen grabbed Tilda's hand, pumping it up and down so enthusiastically, her whole arm ached. The last to offer their congratulations was Silviu.

"Well." He smiled and laid a hand on Tilda's shoulder, his blue eyes sharp as he peered into her face. "Are you ready to begin your apprenticeship?"

An apprenticeship. As a powermage. It seemed unbelievable, but Tilda was ready. She nodded.

"Then I will guide you as best I can." Silviu gave Tilda's shoulder a squeeze and let go. He held up the same hand to quieten the applause. When the room was finally quiet, he raised his voice to the balcony. "The welcome made, we seek to continue the task set before us. To take into ourselves the Power bestowed on Issraya through the conduit of the rings. Let us proceed."

As she had done before, in the storm, Tilda reached into the silver haze which had been shimmering above the Ringstone. As soon as she touched her ring, the five familiar coloured strands shot up. This was it—the start of something huge.

One day, she hoped she would be worthy of the title of powermage. In the meantime, she was under no illusion that there was a lot of learning to be done.

Hello again, Tilda, the Power said.

Tilda smiled, shut her eyes, and let the blue light fill her up.

Katherine Hetzel has always loved the written word, but only started writing "properly" after giving up her job as a pharmaceutical microbiologist to be a stay-at-home mum. The silly songs and daft poems she wrote for her children grew into longer stories. They ended up on paper and then published. (*Granny Rainbow,* Panda Eyes, 2014, *More Granny Rainbow,* Panda Eyes, 2015) Her debut novel, *StarMark,* was published by Dragonfeather in June 2016 and her second stand-alone novel, *Kingstone,* in June 2017. She sees herself first and foremost as a children's author, passionate about getting kids reading, but she also enjoys writing short stories for adults and has been published in several anthologies. A member of the online writing community Den of Writers, Katherine operates under the name of Squidge and blogs at Squidge's Scribbles. She lives in the heart of the UK with Mr Squidge and two children.